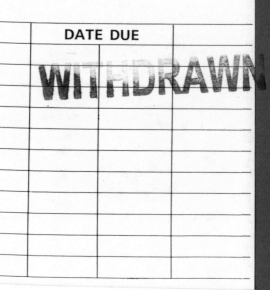

SHADES OF DARK

A CHARLOTTE ZOLOTOW BOOK

SHADES OF DARK

Stories Compiled by Aidan Chambers

Harper & Row, Publishers

Shades of Dark
First published in Great Britain 1984 by Patrick Hardy Books
Copyright © 1984 by Aidan Chambers

The Champions copyright © 1984 by Vivien Alcock;
The Gnomon copyright © 1984 by Jan Mark;
Left in the Dark copyright © 1984 by John Gordon;
Mandy Kiss Mommy copyright © 1984 by Lance Salway;
A Kind of Swan Song copyright © 1984 by Helen Cresswell;
Ivor copyright © 1984 by George Mackay Brown;
The Devil's Laughter copyright © 1984 by Jan Needle;
His Coy Mistress copyright © 1984 by Jean Stubbs.

10 9 8 7 6 5 4 3 2 1
First American Edition

Library of Congress Cataloging-in-Publication Data
Shades of dark.

"A Charlotte Zolotow book."
Contents: The champions / Vivien Alcock — The
gnomon / Jan Mark — Left in the dark / John Gordon —
[etc.]
1. Ghost stories, English. [1. Ghosts—Fiction.
2. Short stories] I. Chambers, Aidan.
PZ5.S5125 1986   [Fic]   85-45840
ISBN 0-06-021247-0
ISBN 0-06-021248-9 (lib. bdg.)

Contents

The Champions

VIVIEN ALCOCK

His name was John Dafte, or as the school register put it, Dafte John. No one made jokes about it. He was a tall, hairy boy, with huge shoulders and long arms and a voice like a big drum. Junior boxing champion, captain of both the cricket and football teams—there wasn't a sport he didn't excel at. We called him, respectfully, Prince Kong.

I admired him tremendously. He was a smiling, good-natured hero, with a strong sense of fair play. He had only to stroll out onto the playground for the bullies to crawl back into their holes.

'Pick someone your own size,' he'd say. (It must have limited *his* choice: there was no one at school anywhere near his size. He dwarfed even the masters.) I thought him a true prince. It didn't worry me that he looked like a gorilla. I *like* gorillas.

On the Monday morning after half term, he came to school with two black eyes, and a split and swollen nose, decorated with dark scabs like beetles.

We crowded round him sympathetically.

'Hey, Prince, you got dark glasses on?'

' 'Ad an argument with a bulldozer, 'ave you?'

'Your mum been beating you up?'

I was not as surprised as the others that he should have come off worst in a fight. I'm good at maths, and can work out that it's no use having the strength of ten, if you happen to pick a quarrel with eleven. It would be just like Prince Kong, I thought, to go charging in to save someone from a gang of toughs, without stopping to count; what did puzzle me was that he should lie about it. I'd

have expected him to smile and say, 'Can't win 'em all.'
Something like that.

Instead he shouldered us roughly out of his way, his
head down, his eyes furtive, muttering furiously,
'Walked into a door.'

'Poor old door, it didn't stand a chance,' I said, and
wished I hadn't when he glared at me. 'Sorry, Prince,' I
said hastily, stepping back. I am thin and, like glass, very
breakable.

We watched him limp into the school building, and
followed at a safe distance, puzzled and a little dismayed.

He and I were in different forms, so I did not see him
again until school was over. I was waiting for one of my
friends when he came down the steps, caught sight of me
and hesitated, staring at me out of his bruised eyes. For
the first time I felt nervous of him, and smiled uneasily.
He limped over and stood looking down at me. A long
way down.

'You're clever, aren't you?' he said.

I thought he was referring to my stupid remark about
the door, and said hastily, 'I'm sorry, Prince. I didn't
mean . . . I was only joking.'

'What?' he asked, puzzled; then shrugged the question away and went on, 'I mean, you come top all the
time. Brainy. Good at working things out—you know,
problems.'

I wriggled my shoulders and replied with regulation
modesty, 'Oh, I dunno. Just lucky, I guess.'

'No. You're clever,' he repeated. I realized suddenly
that he wanted me to be clever. His eyes, between their
swollen, discoloured lids, were gazing at me pleadingly.
If it had been anyone else but Prince Kong, I'd have
thought he was frightened.

'Well . . .' I said—it wasn't the thing to boast, but I
didn't want to let him down—'sort of, I suppose.'

I thought he looked relieved but he did not say anything. The silence became embarrassing.

'Is there . . .? Can I . . .? I mean, if there's anything I can do, just ask,' I mumbled, uneasy beneath his strange, gloomy stare. 'Is it maths? Latin? Not that I'm all that good. . . .' I tailed off.

'Walking home with anybody?' he asked.

'No,' I lied. I could see Mark on the steps, watching us from a respectful distance. I knew he would understand. It was an honour to walk with Prince Kong. Anyone would have jumped at the chance.

'C'n I come with you, then?' he asked. 'Only I got a problem, see?'

'Yes,' I said eagerly. 'Of course.' I didn't see. I couldn't imagine what problem it could be. Not maths or Latin. Prince Kong never worried about his school work. Conscious of his own enormous power, he was content to stay at the bottom. Like a submarine lying low.

'If you tell anybody, I'll skin you,' he said.

'I won't!'

'You'd better not.'

I don't live far enough from the school. Ten minutes later, we were standing outside my home, and still he hadn't told me what it was all about. I don't think he distrusted me. I honestly think he just could not get the words out. He kept turning towards me, opening and shutting his mouth like a giant fish, with nothing coming out but air and a faint smell of onions.

'What's the problem, then?' I asked at last.

But this direct approach seemed to alarm him.

'I dunno,' he mumbled.

We stood in the afternoon sunlight and looked at each other hopelessly.

'Come in and have a Coke?' I suggested.

He hesitated. 'Don't feel like meeting nobody,' he

said. 'Not like this.' He gestured towards his bruised face.

I reassured him that my mother and father were both at work. Wouldn't be back till gone six. I took him indoors, settled him into a chair in our kitchen and poured him a large Coke. Then I sat opposite him, and waited.

He shifted uneasily. 'It's . . .' he began, with that strange frightened look in his eyes. 'It's . . .' He paused. I could almost hear the levers creaking in his head as he changed lines. 'It's me maths,' he finished, looking at me fiercely, challenging me to call him a liar. 'Can't make it out.' He plonked a book on the table, opening it at random. 'All that,' he said, waving a large hand, 'don't mean a thing.'

I was disappointed. I knew he didn't really care a fig for his maths. But no one in their right mind would argue with Prince Kong, so I picked up the book and began to explain it to him. His eyes glazed. His mouth fell open and he sighed. I didn't think he was listening. I bent my head over the book. . . .

Suddenly I heard the noise of his chair scraping on the tiled floor. I looked up and saw he had got to his feet. He looked . . . different. There was a grim, determined look on his face. As I watched, he walked across the kitchen. Quickly. Firmly. With the air of someone who knew where he was going. Walked with his eyes open, slap bang into the wall! His damaged nose hit the painted plaster with a squelchy smack, leaving a smear of blood like jam.

'Prince!' I cried in amazement.

He staggered back, his hands to his bleeding face. I guided him to his chair. Gave him a clean tea-towel soaked in cold water. He pressed it to his nose. Above it, his eyes looked at me miserably, full of fear.

'Shall I ring the doctor?' I asked.

He shook his head.

'Is it your eyes?' I thought perhaps he was suffering from some kind of intermittent blindness. But he shook his head again.

'What is it? What's the matter?'

He took the tea-towel from his face. It was patched with his blood. His nose was dark red and I could almost see it swelling before my eyes.

'Prince, what's the matter?' I asked again.

'You'll laugh.'

'I won't!' I protested, astonished he should think me so heartless.

It was then, at last, that he managed to get the words out.

'I think I've swallowed a ghost.'

I stared at him.

'*What*?'

'Ghost,' he repeated firmly, 'G.H.O.S.T. Spirit. Spook.'

'Oh!'

He looked at me suspiciously. A spasm of suppressed laughter was shaking me. I couldn't help it. It was partly nerves, I think. I shut my mouth firmly and tried to make my face show nothing but sympathetic inquiry.

'It wouldn't have happened,' he said gloomily, 'if I'd kept me mouth shut.'

He told me he had been staying with his aunt and uncle in Bell Green during the holidays. One night, after supper, they'd got to talking about ghosts. 'You know the way it is,' he said. 'Everybody knows someone who's seen one.' His aunt had told them there was a ghost in Bell Green. She hadn't seen it herself, but lots of people had. When the moon was full, it came out of the river, white as mist, and drifted over the fields at night, howling. . . .

'Sheila, that's me cousin, she laughed and said she bet

that's all it was. Mist and wind and moonlight. But auntie wouldn't have it. For one thing, she said it always come up at the same spot. By the bridge near the old timber mill. A man had drowned himself there once, years ago . . . "Most like fell in when he was drunk," I said, teasing her. She got quite cross. "Why don't you go and see for yourselves," me uncle said, winking at me. "It's a nice night for a walk." '

So they had gone out, Prince Kong and his cousin Sheila, strolling along the river bank in the moonlight.

'Dunno that we was bothering about the old ghost much,' he said, with a sly smile, 'but then we come to this bridge, and there was the old mill facing us on a bend in the river. "This must be the place," Sheila said, and we leaned on the parapet and looked down. Couldn't make out nothing at first. Just sort of splinters of the moon in the water, and reeds, stiff and black like railings. Then we saw it. A bit of mist, thin as string, rising out of the river. Like a white worm it was, wriggling and squirming. Higher and higher it come till it was level with our faces, no more than a foot away. Then it sort of ballooned out into a face. A man's face. I saw it with me own eyes! Not clear—more like when you've caught a right hook on your chin and you see things a bit hazy. Sheila grabbed hold of me arm, and I . . .well, I sort of drew me breath in sharpish . . . and *swallowed him!* Are you laughing?' he demanded angrily.

'No,' I said quickly. 'Go on.'

'He'd thinned out again, see, and he slipped down me throat like spaghetti. I could feel him all the way down. Cold. Like ice. It was horrible.'

'What did you do?'

'Well, I tried to cough him up, but he wouldn't come. Soon as I got back to auntie's, I went to the bathroom, and stuck me finger down me throat. Sicked up all me supper down the bog. Waste of good food. It didn't do no

good. Frightened him, though,' he said with grim satis-
faction. 'I could feel him scuttling about inside me like an
ice cube on the run. Banging into me ribs, freezing me
heart. . . . He's up here now,' he said, tapping his head.
He gave the ghost of a smile. 'Plenty of room at the top.
I'm not brainy like you.'

'Does it hurt?' I asked curiously.

'Not hurt, exactly. It's just cold. Terribly cold.' He put
his huge red hand on his head as if to warm it. 'It's
numbing me brain. I wouldn't mind so much if the silly
beggar didn't think he could still walk through walls and
closed doors. Look at me dial! That's our kitchen shelf.
That's our front door,' he said, pointing to the various
bruises on his face. 'That's a brick wall. And he's done
me nose five times. Six, counting your wall. Yesterday he
walked me into a No. 210 bus. Lucky I wasn't killed. I
dunno what to do. Every time me mind goes blank, he
does something daft. It's got me beat.'

I no longer felt like laughing. He sat there, his great
head bowed, his strong hands helpless on the table.

'You mustn't let your mind go blank, Prince,' I said.
'You must keep thinking all the time . . .'

'All the time?' he repeated, looking at me with amazement.

'Yes.'

He shook his head. 'Couldn't do it, Mike,' he said
decidedly. 'Not all the time. Out of practice, see? More
used to thinking with me hands and feet. Got a clever
body, Dad says. After all,' he added defensively, 'we
can't all have brains in the same place. No reason why
they got to be in the head, is there?'

'Well,' I said, 'it's more usual.'

'Anyway, what about when I go to sleep? Can't go
without sleep for ever. Got you there.'

I had to admit it. We sat still, trying to think. I was
supposed to be clever, but I have to confess I hadn't an

idea in my head. It was Prince Kong who thought of something first.

'Hit me,' he said suddenly.

'Hit you?'

'Yeah. Here.' He jutted out his granite chin. 'Might jolt him out, see?'

I hesitated.

'Come on. Hit me.'

I clenched my fist. It looked as small and as fragile as a glass bead. We both inspected it dubiously. Prince shook his head.

'Got small hands, haven't you? I reckon the wall hit me harder than you could. Pity. Don't want to bust your knuckles for nothing.'

'Sorry.'

'Not your fault,' he said kindly.

We sat silently again, racking our brains.

'This man, why did he drown himself?' I asked.

'Dunno. Auntie didn't say. Don't matter, does it?'

'I thought it might help if we knew something about him.'

Prince brightened. 'Yeah. Study his form. Find out whether he favours the right or the left. . . .' He looked despondent again. 'Don't see how it helps with a ghost, though.'

'Does he walk every night?'

'No. Full moon, auntie said.'

'I wonder where he was the rest of the time.'

'Dunno. Back in the river, I suppose.'

The river. . . .

'Bell Green is in Hertfordshire, isn't it?' I asked.

'Yeah.'

'North of here?'

'Yeah.'

I pointed to the smear of blood on the wall. 'That's north,' I said.

He looked puzzled. 'What are you getting at?'

'Perhaps he's trying to get back to the river. Perhaps he just wants to go home. Look, let's go there—it's not far, is it? You could open your mouth over the water and let him out. It's worth trying.'

He looked at me admiringly. 'I said you was clever, Mike.'

I beamed. I really thought I was clever. You see, I didn't really believe in the ghost. I'd stopped believing in ghosts when I was six. I thought it was all his imagination. Perhaps in his last fight he'd been hit too hard on his head and was still a bit punch drunk. That, and the moonlight and the mist. All I had to do, I thought, was to convince him I'd seen the ghost come out of his mouth and plop into the river . . . must get him to shut his eyes . . . throw a stone into the water to make a splash. . . .

'Trust me, Prince,' I said smugly. Fool that I was.

It was only half-past five. I left a note for my mother saying I was going to supper with a friend, and would be back lateish. We took the tube to Barnet, and then caught a bus to Bell Green.

The light was fading when we came to the bridge, and the river looked cold and dirty. Tall nettles grew up the banks.

'Shall we go right down to the water?' Prince asked.

I looked at the nettles.

'No. Just as good from here. Can you still feel him?'

He nodded and tapped his head. 'Here,' he said.

'Lean over the bridge and shut your eyes,' I instructed.

'Shut me eyes? Why?'

'Er . . . to help your mind go blank,' I improvised. 'You said that's when he did things.'

Obligingly, Prince leaned over the parapet, his head hanging down, his mouth open, eyes shut. I bent down and picked up a small stone. But before I could toss it into the water, he groaned suddenly and straightened up.

'What's the matter?' I asked.

'Oh my God, oh my God!' he cried, with terrible anguish, and turned his face towards me. I backed away, staring. His face was moving, twitching, jerking, as if a battle was taking place beneath the skin.

'Prince!' I shouted, terrified. 'Prince!'

'Oh my God!' he said again, and his voice was utterly different, unfamiliar.

'John!' I cried, using his real name for the first time. 'John Dafte! *Come back!*'

For a moment I thought I saw the boy I knew looking out of the bruised eyes. Then his face changed again.

'God help me,' the ghost groaned. Blundering past me, he left the bridge, stumbled down through the nettles to the water's edge and threw himself in.

I ran after him, slipping on the steep bank, stinging my hands. He was thrashing about in the water, his fists flailing as if he were fighting himself.

'Prince! Prince, you can swim! You're the champion, remember?' I shouted. I slipped off my shoes, and was tearing off my anorak and trousers. 'Swim, Prince! Swim to the bank!'

I don't know if he heard me. He put his arms above his head and disappeared.

I dived in. The water was so cold. And dark. I could not see him. I swam desperately backwards and forwards, feeling about with my hands. Once I thought I had hold of his hair and pulled, but it was only weeds.

'Please, God, let me find him!' I prayed.

Suddenly his huge figure rose up in front of me, face pale in the dim light, wild eyes staring. I swam up to him, but he lashed out with his arm and knocked me away in a boil of bubbles. Then he was gone again.

I dived into the widening circle of ripples, spreading my arms under the water. My hand caught hold of cloth, an arm . . . I pulled. He did not fight me this time. He could not. I towed him to the river's edge and slid his heavy body onto a patch of mud and reeds. I could not lift him onto the bank.

He was not breathing.

I turned his head to one side, and pulled his slimy tongue forward, trying desperately to remember what I knew about the kiss of life. Then I put my mouth over his, and breathed as hard as I could. His lips tasted of mud and foul water, and were horribly cold. In and out, I breathed into his massive lungs, in and out, in and out. I was crying, my tears falling on his wet face. In and out, in and out.

He's dead, I thought, I've killed him.

Then suddenly his chest heaved. He breathed in, emptying my lungs till I felt like a vacuum flask. Then breathed out again, air and water, cold as ice. Now he was coughing and choking, spitting out great mouthfuls of the river onto the mud and reeds, while I thumped him on the back, laughing and crying, happier than I had ever been before.

An hour later, we were sitting in borrowed pyjamas, wrapped in blankets, by his aunt's gas fire in Bell Green. A passing truck and two strong farmers had heard my shouts and come to our rescue.

'Your mum and dad are coming right over, Mike,' she told me. She put her hand on my forehead, and frowned. 'You're shivering, yet you feel hot. I hope you haven't caught a chill. Funny, it was our Johnny that near drowned, yet he's almost got over it. While you . . .'

'I'm all right,' I said.

'I'm going to make up a bed for you,' she decided. 'I don't think you're fit to go home tonight. I don't like the look of you at all.' She smiled, and kissed the top of my head. 'You saved our Johnny's life,' she said. 'We got to take good care of you.'

When she had left the room, Prince Kong looked at me anxiously.

'You bad?' he asked.

'No.'

'Want the fire up higher?'

'No, I'm hot.'

'You're shivering.'

'I know.'

'You haven't caught something, have you?'

'Yes!' I shouted unhappily. 'I've caught your bleeding ghost!'

There was a pause. Then he said slowly, 'You gave me the kiss of life, didn't you?'

I nodded.

'And that's when . . .?'

'When you breathed out,' I said, 'I had my mouth open.'

He frowned. 'Where is he?' he said fiercely.

I put my hand on my head. 'Here.'

'Like a cube of ice?'

'Yes.'

'Sort of numbing your brain?'

'Yes.' My voice shook. 'I'll never get my "O" levels now,' I said miserably.

Another silence. Then Prince got to his feet.

'Stand up, Mike,' he said with so much authority that I stood up immediately, looking at him in bewilderment.

'Sorry, mate,' he said. I saw it coming; a huge fist shooting towards me. My head exploded. Everything went red. Green. Black.

Well, here I am, a hero, in hospital with a broken jaw. Everyone makes a fuss of me. Prince Kong came to visit me this afternoon, tiptoeing over the polished floor of the ward, a pile of comics under his arm.

He sat down on the chair by my bed and looked at me anxiously.

'Has he gone?' he asked.

I couldn't talk, of course. I was done up like a Christmas parcel. So I put my thumb up.

He beamed. 'A knock-out,' he said happily. Then he took hold of my hands, and very gently moved them above my head and put them together.

'What on earth are you doing?' a nurse asked, coming up.

Prince clasped his own hands above his head, and shook them.

'We're the champions!' he said.

The Gnomon

JAN MARK

Handsome Daniel Maddison strolled through the hall of the Golden Wheel Guest House and chanced on a mirror that hung near the reception desk.

'Dan loves mirrors,' his sister Clare had once said. 'He can look at them for hours.' He permitted himself a sidelong glance in passing, but halted when he heard his mother chatting in the coffee lounge with Mrs Glover, the proprietor. They were apparently discussing Daniel.

'Honestly,' said Mrs Maddison, 'you'd never think he was nearly sixteen.'

Daniel and his reflection nodded to each other in tacit agreement. They could easily pass for eighteen, and often did.

'Sometimes he behaves like a five-year-old.' Daniel scowled and moved closer to the door of the coffee lounge, the better to hear Mrs Glover's reply. Mrs Glover, schooled by years of discreet hospitality, spoke always with restraint, but it was Mrs Newcombe, a fellow guest, who answered his mother. Mrs Newcombe communicated through a built-in loud hailer.

'I'd never have suggested it, if I'd thought he'd mind,' Mrs Newcombe yelled, elegantly.

'Just one afternoon he's been asked to give up, out of his entire holiday, and he's been sulking since breakfast,' said Mrs Maddison. 'Still, he's not going to upset poor Susie; I'll see to that.'

Daniel's afternoon, which had been scheduled to include a naughty film at the ABC in town on the strength of his easily passing for eighteen, was to be sacrificed in the interests of lolloping Susie Newcombe from Leighton Buzzard who wanted to explore certain atmospheric ruins, a squalid pile of hard core on a nearby hillside, and dignified as an ancient monument solely by the presence of a plaque erected by the Department of the Environment. Daniel's services as escort and guide had been rashly offered, and lacking his permission, by his mother who, without sharing it, liked to boast about his knowledge of archaeology. Both Maddisons and Newcombes had arrived at the Golden Wheel on the same day, but by adroit programming Daniel had avoided meeting Susie after the first confrontation at dinner on the evening of their arrival. This unfortunate introduction during which, after a day spent travelling, neither of the parties was at their best, had sealed Susie's fate as far as Daniel was concerned.

'I love old places like this,' Susie had said, gesturing at the low ceilings and murky nooks of the Golden Wheel's dining-room. 'I think this place is really spooky, don't you? Don't you?' Daniel remained silent and savaged his rhubarb crumble. 'Don't you think it's spooky?'

'Not particularly,' Daniel said. He detested words like spooky, eerie, spine-chilling; also weird, incorrectly used. 'Just decrepit,' he said flatly.

'But doesn't it make you *feel* weird?' Susie persisted. 'I felt something, the moment I came in.'

'I bet you did,' Daniel mouthed, under the pretence of chewing rhubarb crumble.

'They've got a ghost,' Clare chipped in. 'I asked.'

'I know. It's really weird how you can tell, isn't it?' Susie said. 'Mrs Glover said it was a girl who crept out one day to meet her lover and he never turned up. Mrs Glover said she's still waiting.'

'Has she seen her?'

'Nobody's seen her,' Susie breathed. Crumbs flew. 'Apparently you just sort of feel her, sort of waiting.'

'*Weird.*'

'And you can smell roses. She was carrying roses.'

'Has Mrs Glover ever smelled roses?'

'Yes. You can sometimes smell them even in winter. She said, if you ever smell roses, you'll know Maud's about— that was her name, this ghost; Maud Ibbotson.'

'You'd have a job not to smell roses at this time of year,' Daniel observed, looking out of the window at the July sun, low in the sky and flooding with rich colour the rose garden that lay beyond the windows.

'If I smell roses I shall *faint*,' Susie remarked, allowing the skin in the jug of custard to flop like a flexible frisbee over her second helping of rhubarb crumble.

'It's really eerie, isn't it?' Clare said. 'A ghost you can only smell. What happened to her, this Maud? Did she die of a broken heart, or something?'

'Oh no, I asked Mrs Glover. She said there was an accident. She had a fall, or something, while she was waiting, and when they found her it was too late to do anything, and she died.'

'A fall? Out of a window?'

'I expect so. She'd be leaning out to look for him, wouldn't she? I wonder which one it was?' Susie looked round speculatively at the dining-room windows, and sniffed.

'I bet if we found it we should be able to feel something,' Clare said.

Susie shuddered pleasurably. 'Let's try. I've never seen a ghost, but I often *feel* things.'

It was in order to commune with the past that Susie wished to explore the ruins that afternoon, in Daniel's company. Susie would feel less weird in Daniel's company, according to Daniel's mother. 'I thought feeling weird was the object of the exercise,' said Daniel, but to no avail. He put his head round the door of the coffee lounge and flashed a hideous smile across his face, like a neon advertisement in Piccadilly Circus.

'Where are you off to?' Mrs Maddison asked, with base suspicion.

'To wait for Susie,' Daniel said, affronted. Did she really think he was such a fool as to sneak off to the cinema? 'I'll be in the rose garden—will you tell her when she comes down?'

He was not lying. He fully intended to wait for Susie in the rose garden but, so far as he knew, neither Susie nor his mother was aware that at the Golden Wheel there were two rose gardens; the one at the back, beyond the dining-room, and the other one. Daniel was going to wait in the other one.

He had discovered the second garden by accident while evading, as it happened, an earlier encounter with spooky Susie and her chilly spine. The official rose garden was broad and spacious with standard trees in circular beds, a blanched statue or two, and little white iron tables and chairs disposed here and there on the clipped turf. It reminded him of a crematorium. Along one side was a low rockery hedged with conifers that had had their tops nipped off in adolescence. Resolutely squaring their shoulders they now formed an im-penetrable windbreak.

'They're pleached,' said Mrs Newcombe, and with her daughter's vampire ability to fasten onto a harmless word and bleed it white, she repeated it at intervals, liking the sound of it. 'Pleached.' It described her voice very accurately, Daniel thought. He could hear her pleaching now as he slipped away from the house, crossed the lawn beyond the dining-room windows, and sidled between the cypress boughs of the conifer hedge, into the other rose garden.

He guessed that before the conifers were planted and the rockery raised, it had been an extension of the main garden, but now the windbreak obscured it entirely. Daniel, who had originally squeezed between the trees in an effort at hasty concealment, had been amazed to find himself in an open space instead of being, as he had expected, compressed between the conifers and a wall. Today he muttered, 'Open, sesame,' and passed straight through to stand at the head of the second rose garden. Unlike the public part, it seemed to exist for the sole purpose of growing roses. It was narrow. Heavy banks of pink blossoms, one could scarcely call them mere flowers, overhung a trellis on either side, and shaded lush grass that had been cut, but not recently. Yellow ramblers rambled; cream climbers rioted. At the far end was a wooden rustic seat, weathered to the shade of old pewter, and at the nearer, close to where he stood, was the only other furniture, a sundial. Daniel had expected to find an inscription on its bronze plate, *Tempus fugit* perhaps, and there was one, but not *Tempus fugit*. *Time and the hour run through the roughest day*, it said in Roman letters that encircled the Roman numerals. Daniel, recognizing the quotation, took it to mean that everything must come to an end if you wait long enough. The gnomon pointed at his back as he walked down the garden to the rustic seat.

'Come into the garden, Maud,' said Daniel, the scent of roses clogging his flared nostrils, and suddenly suspected that it was here, and not in the house, that Miss Ibbotson had come to her tryst. He waited for the sensation that ought to chill his spine as it certainly would have chilled Susie's. If Susie were there, would Maud Ibbotson manifest herself as she waited for her faithless lover who was now, according to Clare's researches, one hundred and twelve years overdue? He imagined her standing by the rustic seat, tall, stately, leaning several degrees from the perpendicular and counterbalanced by a bustle, like an old joke in *Punch*. She would be no joke if he did see her, but no one ever had seen her. They only smelled roses.

Daniel sat down on the rustic seat, propped his feet on the farther arm and settled back to read and yawn. Distantly, mercifully diminished by distance, Mrs Newcombe pleached on. From time to time the telephone rang in the reception hall, but in the rose garden, regardless of the sundial's admonition, time hung suspended. The roses, ripe for disintegration, nevertheless remained whole. Not a petal fell to the ground. Beyond the hedge a strident shriek, fit to chill the hardiest spine, split the gentle air.

'Danie-elll!'

He looked down discouragingly at his book.

'*Danie-elll!*' The voice advanced, receded, advanced again. Daniel, rather than look at the hedge in case Susie felt his penetrating gaze and discovered him, fastened his eyes upon the nearest rose, a swollen globe of lingerie pink, like something off a chorus girl's garter. He stared at it.

'Danie-el!'

Over-examined, the rose blurred and softened before his eyes, but when he refocused it was still there, and the voice, a little subdued, receded disconsolately towards the house. 'Danny?' Daniel's left forefinger reached out and tipped the rose under the chin, but even now, on the point of dissolution, it remained on its stem.

'Daniel?' It was his mother's voice, sharpened by anger to Mrs Newcombe's pitch, and like a harpy echo Mrs Newcombe joined in. 'Daniel?'

'I'm not here, dear,' Daniel murmured. He heard their conversation in angular duet, his mother embarrassed and apologetic, Mrs Newcombe making light of things, but maternal, affronted on Susie's behalf. She and Mrs Maddison were already on Pat and Shirley terms.

'Oh Shirley, I'm *so* sorry. I can't think . . .'

'It's not *your* fault, Pat.'

The telephone rang again. Daniel glanced up and saw the rose's soft sphere glowing at the very edge of his eyesight. When he reached the end of the chapter he would allow himself the pleasure of beheading that foolish, nodding flower if it did not fall before he was ready for it.

Mrs Newcombe pleached unexpectedly close to the conifer hedge. Daniel's eyes were drawn unwillingly towards it, twin lasers drilling into the back of her crimped head through the dense branches (Go away, you old bat. Hop off.) and saw, near the sundial, a rose explode silently in a shower of pink petals. Daniel stared and absorbed what he had seen. It appeared that the rose had not so much dropped as *burst*. A little closer, the same thing happened again; a second rose vanished and this time the petals did not fall down, but flew up, as if a hand had clouted the rose from below. Daniel closed his own itching forefinger against his palm and saw a third rose evaporate. At the same time he felt his trouser leg stir against his shin, a web of hair unravel across his forehead. Waiting for his own rose to drop, as it surely must now that the wind had found its way into the garden, Daniel swung his feet to the ground and felt a current of air round his ankles, too low to fell a rose; and then, on the far side of the garden, a fourth blossom erupted with such violence that the petals were knocked into the foliage and lodged there. Not one reached the grass. Three blooms in close conference on one stem were struck apart. Daniel watched the drifting confetti and pondered upon the word *struck*. It was almost, Daniel thought, as if someone were walking round the garden and striking at the roses as he went: as she went: there . . . there . . . and *there*: someone who was waiting, and had tired of waiting, tired of roses. Now a dozen died together under a downward blow that dashed them to pieces, while a lateral swipe at another spray sent petals flying against Daniel's face, three metres distant.

Now she is using both hands, Daniel thought. Left and right—oh, our patience is *exhausted*, isn't it?

There was no wind in the adjacent garden where, over the tops of the conifers, Daniel could see a crack willow weeping its burden to the ground. Just beside him, fragments of his own rose took to the air and he heard the soft thud as it broke up. It was fearfully close.

Here she comes, said Daniel, not noticing that he had closed his book and now sat on the very edge of the rustic seat, one arm flexed against the silky wood to thrust himself upright. Here she comes. Not yet impelled to run, she strode, skirt sweeping the turf, beside one trellis, across to the other, across, along, and as she went her arm swung up and *there*, another rose gone, and another, and a whole blasted bouquet, there, there, and *there*.

Daniel drew in his feet as the imperious air swept by him. She was moving faster now, there, there, and *here*. Not a rose escaped that was ripe, and now she was laying into the half-blown flowers, tearing them alive from the branches, not pausing to crush them but flinging them behind her, grabbing at the next while the last was still airborn, arcing and diving. The grass was dappled all over, not only below the trellises, with pink and cream and yellow bruises. She tore at the very stems, twisting and ripping them from the briars. They were not thornless roses. Her hands were surely shredded, blood running down her scything arms to the elbow. And flayed to the bone as she must be, still she flung from one side to the other, wrenching and rending until even the buds were broken and hung down, dead before they were alive, as she cast herself from side to side, there, there and *there*.

And then she stopped, wrecked, and let her bleeding

arms dangle. Daniel, straining to see the thing he must avoid, lifted himself from the seat and began to edge across the grass towards the shelter of the trellis, eyes everywhere to see where the next rose would fall. But there was no next rose. In all the garden there was not one bloom intact, no living thing left to destroy.

Except me, said Daniel, and the air struck him in the face and spun him round so that he fell back against the seat and slithered to the ground, his head aching from side to side as though it were an arm that had felled him. He saw the grass creep and gleam, under pressure, as the tempest wrapped him round, in awful, forceful silence, and dragged him to his feet.

'No!' Daniel shouted. 'Not me, not me. I never kept you waiting.' He wrestled with the wind that surged and sucked at him until he began to stumble down the garden towards the sundial, with cold arms about his neck, cold skirts flapping about his legs, and a frozen face against his cheek. He thought she must throw him out of her garden, neck and crop, to punish him for keeping a poor girl waiting. But he soon saw that although he and she were headed for the conifers, before them, directly in his path, stood the sundial.

'No!' he shouted again, and leaned back against the wind that all at once gathered behind him and pushed, with horrible confidence, so that the slippery soles of his shoes skated over the grass and petals towards the stone column, the bronze dial, the shining gnomon. 'No,' he said, 'no!' But a colder breath than his stopped the cry in his mouth, and a final thrust sent him reeling, headlong. His foot came down heavily on the greasy roses, turning his ankle, and he fell flat, on the grass, and at the same time heard a hissing whistle of breath that choked and stopped, bubbled, and died away. He lay at the foot of the sundial, one hand to his forehead where he had gashed it against the plinth, and looking up saw the gnomon pierce the cloudless sky, just where his heart would have been had his skid not thrown him to one side. It glistened wetly in the dry, still air.

After a long time he raised himself from the turf and crawled away through the conifers to the garden of the Golden Wheel, where his mother and Mrs Newcombe were spreading crockery and cakes on a little white iron table. They both turned round simultaneously and converged with shrill cries, hauling him upright.

'Where've you *been*?' his mother demanded. Daniel pointed vaguely.

'In there.'

'In where?'

'There.'

'What are you talking about? Oh look, Shirley, his head. Daniel, what have you done?'

'The rose garden,' Daniel said. 'Don't go in the rose garden.'

'This is the rose garden. What is he talking about?'

'Wandering,' said Mrs Newcombe, wisely, mouth pursed. 'You ought to get him inside to lie down, Pat. Can't be too careful with knocks on the head, especially just there.'

Mrs Glover came towards them across the starry grass.

'An accident? Oh my, what's all this?' She took Daniel by the chin and examined his forehead. 'That's a nasty one. Where did you get that?'

'In the rose garden, he says. I can't imagine what happened,' Mrs Maddison was saying. 'We just looked round and saw him lying over there, by the rockery. I can't get any sense out of him. He just keeps saying he was in the rose garden, but he wasn't, of course. *We* were. I can't think how he got there without anyone seeing him, and I can't get him to say what hit him. It looks like something sharp—right-angled, almost. Like the corner of something.'

'Not this rose garden . . . that one.' He tried to raise an arm to show them, but they bore him indoors and made him lie down on the cretonne covered settee in the coffee lounge.

'*I* thought he came out through the conifer hedge,' said Mrs Newcombe.

'Oh.' Mrs Glover looked so dismayed that the twittering conference fell silent. 'Oh dear, *that* rose garden. Oh no, he shouldn't have gone in there.'

'You mean there *is* another?' Mrs Maddison rounded on Daniel. 'I suppose you were trespassing.'

'Not trespassing.' Mrs Glover hurried to intervene. 'But we don't use it any more. It gets so windy.' She looked at him. 'Is that what happened, dear? It got windy?'

He nodded. Mrs Newcombe swooped over him with an icy dripping flannel and swabbed his forehead.

'Oh, nonsense. There hasn't been a breath of wind all day,' Mrs Maddison cried, vexed and put out. She hated scenes, especially scenes of Daniel's engineering.

'It's a funny place, that little garden,' Mrs Glover said. 'That's why we hedged it off. It seems to act as a kind of funnel. You get quite strong winds in there, even when it's still everywhere else.' She laughed, almost apologetically. 'Our little tempests, we call them.'

Daniel thought of the wreckage that this little tempest had left behind it. He opened one eye and saw Mrs Glover looking at him. She telegraphed to him: *I know what you were doing in there, young man, and serve you right.*

He answered: *It's happened before, hasn't it? You ought to put up a wall.*

Mrs Newcombe was pleaching again. 'He looked as if he'd seen a ghost.'

'I didn't see anything,' Daniel said, weakly. They came over to him and leaned down, all concern.

'Can you remember what happened, yet?' Mrs Maddison asked. 'Did you have a fall?'

Yes, I had a fall, just like Maud. Maud had a fall, too. Do you know what she fell *on*?

'I was just reading,' said Daniel, 'and waiting for Susie.'

'Susie was waiting for *you*,' his mother retorted, asperity eroding sympathy.

'Where is she?'

'She went out with Clare, in the end. She got tired of waiting.'

'She wasn't the only one,' Daniel whispered, and turned his face to the cretonne back of the settee, to escape the slight smile that curled Mrs Glover's prim lips. In the end they gave up grilling him and left him to his own devices.

'A little sleep won't do any harm,' said Mrs Newcombe.

When they had gone, back to their tea at the white iron table, Daniel sat up gingerly, and looked through the window towards the conifer hedge, behind which, among the scent of roses, Maud Ibbotson was still waiting, so angry, so desperate for company, her patience worn so dangerously thin.

Left in the Dark

JOHN GORDON

The village seemed to be stitched into the hills. A cluster of houses was held by the thread of the stream, and the stream itself was caught under a bridge and hooked around a stone barn in a fold of the heather and bracken. In the October sunshine the hills looked as soft as a quilt.

'There it is,' said the big lady sitting in front of the bus near the driver. 'Lastingford.'

'Me Mam'll never remember that,' said Alec to Jack alongside him. 'She'll never have room to get it on the envelope.'

'It's worse than that, man,' said Jack. 'I don't suppose they even get the post out here.'

The lady had heard them and she stood up and turned round so that she could talk to the whole bus. 'Now I don't want any of you to get worried,' she said. 'The people here are just the same as anywhere else and I know they're going to make you welcome.' She smiled down at Alec and Jack. 'And you'll all be hearing from home because the post comes quite regularly.'

David, sitting by himself behind the other two, wanted her to look at him. She had been standing by the bus in Newcastle, ticking their names off on her list and watching as his Mam kissed him and his Dad shook his hand. Her rather large face under the green hat with the brim had had the funny little smile that women gave before they burst into tears, and she had nodded to his mother, who was quite unable to speak, as he climbed aboard. But now she had gone bossy, nursing her clipboard like a baby, so he looked out of the window again, and carefully, so that nobody else could see, took the tears away from the corners of his eyes with his fingertips.

'Missus.' Jack got the lady's attention. 'Do they ever have bombs here?'

'No, of course they don't. That's why you're being evacuated. You'll be as safe as houses.'

David had seen a house come down. Half an hour after a bomb had landed, while the men in white helmets were climbing over fallen walls and jagged wood, the house next door had collapsed with its grey slates sliding like molten slag, and the smoke from the kitchen fire still coming from the chimney pot as it plunged in a gentle roar into the soft cloud of dust. Mrs Armstrong was dead under that, but he never saw her.

'So you've got nothing to worry about,' said the lady. 'There'll be cows and milk and horses.'

'And duck ponds?' Alec, with the very pale face and bright red hair, looked up at her innocently. 'With little ducks?'

She was not sure whether he was making fun of her, and blushed as she said, 'I wouldn't be surprised. You're in the countryside now, you know.'

'I love fluffy little ducks,' said Alec, and the lady pretended not to see as he and Jack put their heads together and choked to stop themselves laughing. She walked past them to the back of the bus.

That smaller boy, she thought, the one behind them, he wouldn't mind talking about ducks. But I can't say anything to him or they'll think he's a baby. Well he's not much more. She looked at her clipboard. He's only eight. She shook her head. It was bad enough for the other two, and they were three or four years older, but the little one should never be away from home.

They were going down into the valley now, but David could still see the hills humped like the green eiderdown on his bed at home where, first thing in the morning, he

made landscapes of it and had adventures up and down
its slopes.

The bus stopped in the mouth of a stony track between
the pub and a shop that looked more like a house with all
the goods stacked inside somebody's front room. There
were two Boy Scouts on the bus, big lads who had come
to help with the evacuees, and they were each given their
own little group to shepherd, but the lady picked out
Alec and Jack and David to come along with her. 'These
three are together,' she told the Scouts. 'I'll just see them
settled first.' And then she raised her voice so that
everybody could hear. 'I'll be along to see every one of
you and make sure you're all nice and comfy.' But some
of the girls were crying. 'It's just like a holiday,' she said.
'The people here are really looking forward to having
you. You'll see.' She looked up and down the steep road.
One woman stood on her doorstep a little way down the
street; otherwise there was nobody.

'Missus.' Jack caught the lady's attention. 'I've never
been on holiday.'

A desperate gleam crossed her face. 'Never mind,' she
said. Her voice had a tremble in it and her accent slipped so
that she spoke like their mothers. 'Don't worry, pet, I'm
going to take you to a really nice house. Now pick up
your things.'

Jack had his clothes in a parcel, but Alec and David
each had small suitcases, Alec's with a strap around it,
and all three wore overcoats despite the heat of the
October sun. They had come to stay, and winter was not
far away.

The lady led them uphill and around a sharp corner
into a rough road which climbed away steeply to the high
hillside where sheep were placed like puffs of anti-
aircraft smoke among the purple heather, but they
turned sharply again, and a few paces took them to the
front of a tall, plain-faced house of grey stone. Plants

with broad leaves stood in the windows on each side of the door, and lace curtains hung like rain falling in the dark rooms behind. But the brass door knocker was brightly polished and the step was scrubbed almost white. The lady's hand was still reaching for the knocker when the door opened, pulled suddenly back, and a girl of about sixteen stood there, trying to see beyond the upstretched arm and at the same time saying, 'Hallo, have you brought them—the evacuees? There should be three, all little lads, Mrs Prosser said. Oh yes.'

As the words came tumbling out, her eyes had been alighting on each of them in turn, and counting. 'Good. They're all there.' Her round face beamed.

Her rosy cheeks and quick smile seemed to David to shine against the grey stone and dark hall behind her, and to be quite wrong for the clothes she wore. She had a white lace cap on her brown hair, which was drawn back into a bun, and she wore a black dress buttoned high at the neck, black stockings, and black low-heeled shoes so that her body seemed in a prison from which only her face, looking over the wall, was free. She bobbed a brief curtsey to the lady. 'Mrs Prosser says I'm to take them up to their room while she sees you in the parlour.'

The lady in the green hat stood to one side and let them go ahead of her, touching each on the shoulder as they went by as though what she really wanted to do was hold them back because they were barging into a place where they did not belong. 'Wipe your feet,' she said three times, once to each of them, and then came in behind them and stood quite still, clutching her clipboard, as the maid closed the door and shut out most of the light. The hall was dim and chilly.

Jack sniffed. 'Smells of polish,' he said. 'Look at the shine on that floor.'

A thin rug lay along the centre of the hall and Alec pushed at it with his toe so that it wrinkled over the polished wood. 'Could be dangerous if you came down-stairs in a rush,' he said.

Jack also pushed at the carpet. 'Man!' he said loudly, 'you could go arse over tip on that!'

'Sh!' The lady was horrified, but the girl gave a little strangled squeak and went past them with her lips and eyes squeezed tight. She opened a door and they heard her mumble something and then hastily beckon the lady forward, show her through, and shut the door quickly behind her.

'You lot!' She held herself very upright, struggling not to laugh. 'If that's the way you're going to carry on you'll get me shot. Where's your manners?'

'But it's true,' said Jack. 'That floor's a danger.'

'And it's not the only thing that's dangerous around here.' She advanced on them, and her laughter was now well under control. 'If you don't watch your step, Mrs Prosser will get you sent away home again.'

'I won't mind,' said Jack.

'Nor me neither.' Alec backed him up.

'But what's to become of me?' She had her hands on her hips. 'If you gang don't watch your p's and q's, I'll get the blame and she'll get rid of me, and then what would I do without a job?' She looked at each of them as sternly as her round face would allow. 'Eh?'

David saw that the other two were going to stand dumbly, and he was suddenly afraid they would turn the one friendly face against them. 'We won't get you into trouble, Miss,' he said.

He stood partly behind the others and was the smallest. Her eyes rested on him fully for the first time and her expression suddenly melted. 'You don't call me Miss,' she said. 'I'm not old enough for that.'

Jack turned and looked down at David. 'Everybody knows that,' he said. 'Don't be daft.'

'No he's not.' The girl seemed suddenly to charge at

them. 'He's not daft. He's the nicest little lad of the three of you. What's your name, pet?'

'David,' he said.

'Right then, David. We'll lead the way and let them follow.' She held out her hand and he longed to hold it but he knew that if he did the others would call him soft, so he stood firm and looked up at her sternly. Once again she had to hold back a giggle. 'Very well then, David,' she said, and turned to the other two to get their names. 'You can call me Pauline, but you better not be cheeky, or else I'll tell the Missus.'

She turned, and her face and cap were hidden so that her figure was entirely black and merged with the deep shadows at the end of the hall so completely that David thought she had vanished through some side doorway. Only the rustle of her dress drew him forward. Then she was climbing stairs much broader than in any house in his own street, and he hurried forward in case she should disappear again. She climbed swiftly and his heavy case bumped against his legs as he struggled to keep up with her. But when they came to a landing she waited for them. 'Are you out of puff?' she said. 'Because we've got a long way to go yet.'

There was a window with coloured glass. 'It's just like being in a church,' Jack said to her.

'And nearly as cold.' Alec shivered. 'Do you have hymns?'

'No music.' Pauline shook her head. 'The Missus doesn't like to hear anybody singing. She doesn't like any noise at all inside these four walls.'

The unseen Mrs Prosser could hardly have complained as they mounted the next flight and the next because the chatter from Alec and Jack died out as they became breathless, and the only sound was their feet on the stair carpet. But David noticed that as they climbed higher, and the noise was less likely to be heard down below, the carpet became thinner and their footsteps louder. And the stairway became narrower until there was scarcely enough room for them and their luggage, and their free hands were holding a painted rail. They came to a landing of bare boards and one small window.

'Can't be any farther, can it?' said Jack. 'We must be practically under the roof with the birdies.'

'That's where you're wrong, hinny.' Pauline imitated his Newcastle accent. 'There's one more stage yet.' She went to a plain door that had a latch instead of a handle. 'Lift the sneck,' she said as she raised the latch and pulled back the door, 'and here we are. Almost.'

She went into darkness and they heard her feet on the wooden treads of uncarpeted stairs, and then another door opened and let down a grey light on the last flight. 'Come on,' she called, and Jack pushed to the front. Alec did not want to be left on the bare landing and went next, leaving David where he was.

The door swung to and he was suddenly alone. The landing was like a little room, an empty cupboard, and no sound came from below or above, not even the scratch of a beetle. He had had a dream like this, an empty room in a house far away from anything he knew. He stood where he was and waited to wake up.

It was a full minute before Pauline, realizing he was left behind, came clattering down the stairs.

'Oh, poor little lad!' She was immediately alongside him, bending over with her arm around his shoulders. 'You'll break my heart, you will.' Her tears came to the surface but did not quite brim over. 'Standing there with your overcoat buttoned up and your case by your side. You look as though you're all alone on a railway station— little boy lost.' She was suddenly so motherly she even smoothed his dark hair. 'Why didn't you come after us?'

Until then he had not thought of crying, but now his

mouth turned down at the corners. 'There was a man,' he said.

'A man? Where?'

He raised a hand and pointed towards the door. If she hadn't asked him, he was sure he would never have remembered what had just happened. But it was true. A big man had followed Alec through the door, and that was why he had hung back and been left alone.

'There's no man here,' said Pauline. 'Just us.'

'I saw him.' The man was tall and wore a brownish suit.

Pauline studied his face for a moment and then looked carefully around the landing. 'There's no man up here, David. There's no man in the whole house.'

David knew that. But he had seen the broad back and the speckled, rough material of the man's jacket and trousers. It was the sort of thing you see and don't see at the same time, and he would have forgotten it a moment later if it hadn't been for Pauline asking him. She was looking into his face now, as full of kindness as his mother, and his lip quivered.

'Oh,' she said, crouching to hug him, 'it's only your imagination, David, after all you've been through with that horrible Hitler bombing everybody. And we had to go and leave you all by yourself.' She pulled a handkerchief from her sleeve and wiped his eyes. 'But I can tell you this, pet, we'll never leave you alone up here again. Never, ever.'

Mrs Prosser had made sure that the three boys were going to be seen about the house as little as possible. Their room was in the attic, three iron beds in a row under a whitewashed, sloping ceiling.

'Just like a dormitory,' said Jack.

'It's quite nice.' Pauline was straightening bedclothes. 'I've tried to make it homely.' She had brought two rag rugs from home to put on the cold lino and, without Mrs

Prosser knowing, had taken the curtains from another room at the top of the house and hung them in the single dormer window that jutted out from the slates of the roof.

'What's that?' Jack demanded, pointing to a table beneath the window.

'That's a wash-hand-stand. Don't you know anything?' A jug stood in a big basin on the table's marble top. 'That's where you put your soap.' She pointed to a china dish. 'And you hang your towels on these rails around the edge. I'll bring you up some water directly.'

'All of us in the same basin?' Alec didn't believe it. 'The water'll get black.'

'I bags first,' said Jack.

There was a chair with a cane bottom next to a huge wardrobe, but no other furniture. 'You can hang your clothes up in there later,' she told them, 'but now you've got to go and meet the Missus. Put your overcoats on your beds. No . . .' she stopped Jack throwing his coat on the middle bed '. . . that's for the smallest one. You two big lads have got to look after him.' Jack and Alec both pulled faces. 'And you needn't be like that, either.'

'Has he been crying for his Mam?' Jack looked carefully at David's face.

'No I haven't!' David lunged forward suddenly, and Jack had to fend him off as Pauline gave a shriek.

'He's a proper little fury when he's roused.' She was delighted with him. 'You'll have to watch your step.' Jack put his tongue out at her. 'And if there's any more of that you'll have me to deal with.'

'You're only a lass.'

'We'll see about that!' Suddenly she was chasing all three of them round the room and over the beds, until she caught Jack in a corner. 'Say sorry or I'll give you a Chinese burn.' She had her fist bunched ready to scrub her knuckles on his scalp. 'Say sorry!'

'I won't.'

They were struggling and laughing, when faintly, from far away, a bell tinkled. Through all the noise Pauline heard it and instantly pushed herself clear.

'Is my cap straight? Look at my dress—the state it's in! All crumpled up.' She was pushing her hair back and pressing at the creases at the same time. 'Come on now.' Her attitude had changed and she was ordering them to follow her. They even lined up before they went through the door. David was last again, and it was this that made him think of the man. He looked back. The room was quite empty. If there had been a man, the only place he could be was in the wardrobe. David clung to the back of Alec's jacket as he followed him down the stairs.

They came down through the house, their footsteps becoming quieter as the stair carpets thickened, and then they were in the hushed hall. Pauline smoothed her skirt once more, licked her lips, looked briefly at the three boys, and tapped at a door hidden in its own recess. They saw her bob a curtsey as she entered, then stand back and beckon them.

The light coming through the window was guillotined by the drape of the curtains, and when the door closed with a soft click behind him David felt trapped in a dark sea cave. Tall cabinets rose to the ceiling where they lipped over in black scrolls, and pictures in ebony frames leant from the walls like the mouths of great howling creatures held back by chains. His hand reached for Jack's and held it.

'Well?' The voice was a high-pitched yelp, and for a split second he thought he saw a dog in a dress. The grey face against the chair back had high cheekbones and a chin so thin it was like a dog's pointed muzzle. It barked again. 'Stop fidgetting, girl.'

The rustle of Pauline's dress ceased. David had half hidden himself behind Jack as they were lined up on one side of the wide fireplace, and the voice rattled again. 'I can hardly see one of them. Fetch him out.'

Pauline nudged him into the open.

'Are they clean?' The bony eyebrows turned away from them to the lady in the green hat who stood beside her chair.

'Of course they are, Mrs Prosser.' The lady fiddled nervously with her clipboard. 'The nurse looked at their hair before we set out.'

The grey face swung to Pauline. 'Have they got their ration books?'

The lady said, 'I've got them here.'

'Have they been told about wiping their boots?'

'Yes, Mrs Prosser,' lied Pauline.

'And about noise?'

'Yes, Mrs Prosser.'

'You've taken them up and shown them their beds?'

'Yes, Mrs Prosser.'

There was a pause, and the lady said, 'I'm sure they're going to be very comfortable.' She smiled at them. 'Aren't you?'

'We don't know yet,' said Jack.

A sound like the hiss of a serpent came from Mrs Prosser. There was a moment's silence and then the lady beside her started to make excuses, but the grey face leant back with the chin pulled in to the thin neck and the words fell silent. They heard the breath in Mrs Prosser's nostrils before she spoke.

'I want them out of my sight,' she said. 'At once.'

Pauline would not let them say a word until they had climbed to the top of the house.

'Oh,' she said, 'I'll just plonk meself down here till I get me breath back.' She sat in the single chair looking down into her lap and after a moment her shoulders began shaking. It was more than David could bear to see her sobbing and he went and stood in front of her, wanting to touch her but not daring. She looked up and her face was red, but not with tears. She was giggling. 'That young skite Jack,' she said. 'I don't know how he dare!'

David had made a mistake. He tried to grin, but knew there was too much alarm in his face and he tried to move away. Pauline reached and grasped his hand. 'No. Don't go away. Somebody's got to protect me from those two demons.'

'I only spoke the truth,' Jack protested. 'We don't know if we're going to like it yet.' He turned to Alec. 'Do we?'

Alec's pale brow was wrinkled. 'Her downstairs,' he said. 'If that's what *she's* like, what's going to happen when Mr Prosser comes home?'

'Oh hell,' said Jack. 'I hadn't thought.'

'Well you don't need to.' Pauline got to her feet. 'And don't let me hear you using language like that any more.'

'I only said hell.'

'That's enough!' She went briskly to the big wardrobe. 'You don't need worry about Mr Prosser coming home. He's dead.'

'Whew!' Jack let out his breath. 'That was a narrow squeak. I couldn't bear two like that.'

Pauline suddenly turned on him. 'That's just where you're wrong, clever clogs. He wasn't anything like the Missus. Never a bit. Mr Prosser was a lovely man. He was that gentle you felt you always wanted to talk to him, and,' her voice rose, 'I won't have a word said against him.'

Jack was taken aback, but only for a moment. 'But he married *her*,' he said.

Pauline sighed, and they could hear her mother and all the other village women talking as she said, 'It's such a shame they never had any children. But she never would, never in a million years. He wanted them, you could tell that. He was a bit shy like, even with lads and lasses, but he had such a lovely big kind face and eyes just like little Davey's here.' She was teasing now. 'He's going to be a lady-killer, aren't you Davey?'

'I wish you'd shut up,' he said.

'Look, I've made him blush. But it is true, you have got nice big eyes.'

'What about mine?' said Jack.

'You! You're too cheeky by half. Yours are wicked,' and she turned to open the wardrobe door. 'Now here's where you've got to hang your clothes. There's plenty of room.'

'Smells of mothballs,' said Jack, 'and it looks as though somebody's already using it.'

'It's only just one old suit,' she said. 'You three don't look as though you're going to need much space.'

'Whose suit is it?'

Pauline turned to face them. 'It's Mr Prosser's, and I don't want you saying a word about it, any of you, or you'll get me the sack just as sure as night follows day. When he died she made me throw everything out. The lot. Every single thing that was his. I don't think she'd ever wanted him—not him, not children, nothing. All she wants is to sit in state and have the whole village think she's bliddy royalty.'

'Who's swearing now?'

Pauline had reddened. 'Well she makes you. And she wasn't going to have everything her own way, not if I had anything to do with it. So I kept his suit, the old one he wore every day. He used to keep sweets in the pockets for all us kiddies in the village.' She turned back to the open wardrobe. 'Anyway it's still his house and he has a right to be here.'

She reached to move the coat hanger along the rail and, as it slid, the suit swung round so that the back of the jacket was towards them. It was broad and gingery. David had seen it before.

The village school was smaller than the one they were used to, but not so very different. The coke stove had the same breathless fumes, and the blackboard chalk had the same dry taste when you put it on your tongue. Jack found new friends and fought with them in the playground, Alec felt the cold as the winter came on, and David tried to keep up with the big lads and not be homesick, but the ache was with him most of the time.

They hardly ever saw Mrs Prosser. She made sure of that. Once a day a woman came up from the village to cook lunch for her, but they had to stay at school and eat the sandwiches that Pauline made for them. And by the time school was over, and they climbed the hill and turned the corner, the house was bleak and dark and already closed down for the night. Except for the kitchen. They were not allowed to use the front door, and they would not have wanted to, because it was easier to get to the kitchen through the yard at the back, and they knew the fire would still be burning and Pauline waiting for them. David used to think it was like coming out of the dark into a secret burrow with the yellow light of the oil lamp in the centre of the table gleaming on the plates set out for them, and showing the steam curling from the kettle on the hob.

'Something hot,' said Pauline. 'You need it when the nights draw in.' Generally it was soup. 'I'm not the world's best cook,' she said, but she would roast potatoes at the edge of the fire, and bring bread her mother had baked and sent up to the house because she 'couldn't bear the thought of young lads going to bed on an empty stomach'.

It was the best part of the day. They lived in the kitchen, and gradually it began to feel as though they had always been there. The two bigger boys tried to make it belong to them. They never quite succeeded.

They had not been there long when Jack said one

night, 'Where's the wireless? I like that when I'm at home.'

Pauline shook her head. 'We haven't got electricity, and she won't have it in the house anyway.'

'What does she do, then?'

'She sews. She does beautiful embroidery.'

'Her?' He didn't believe it. 'I bet she catches beetles and eats them.'

Pauline laughed, but she hushed him and glanced at the door to the hall. 'You never know where she is,' she whispered. 'She moves so quiet.'

They were noisy enough most nights playing Ludo, which Pauline had brought from home, or they drew pictures, especially David, or sometimes Pauline read to them, mostly stories about murder and love from little books with grey pages she smuggled into the house.

But by seven o'clock the fire was only a few red coals in the grate, and it was time for her to go home and for them to go to bed. Every night she lit a candle and went ahead of them into the dark hall. They moved quietly in the silent house because boots were forbidden and the boys were in their socks. There was always a scuffle because nobody wanted to be last in line with the darkness creeping at their heels as they went higher, and David always lost until Pauline saw what was happening and made either Jack or Alec go alongside him—in case he stumbled, she said.

But still the great whispering well of the stairs surged around them, and the little light made tall shadows lean into walls and doorways and wait for them on the landings above.

'Be quick then,' she always said as she put the candle-stick on the floor and left them as they got undressed. She had to come back, once they were in bed, and take the candle because Mrs Prosser would not allow it to be left. David was clumsy with his clothes, and often she had to help him on with his pyjama jacket, but it gave her the chance to tuck him in which she always wanted to do because he looked so small and forlorn.

'Sleep tight.' She would take one last look around the room and they would see the cracks of light fade around the edges of the door as her steps clattered down the bare stairs.

They huddled under their blankets, talking in the dark about home. David listened. He never said very much, but as the other two talked he walked with them from the lamp post where they always met at nights until the blackout came, and along the street until he saw his mother waiting, and then he realized that his eyes were wet, and his pillow was damp, and he curled tighter and screwed up a corner of the sheet until it was the shape of the limp toy dog he always took to bed at home. He had been afraid to bring it with him.

One night he was almost asleep when Alec said into the darkness, 'I wouldn't like to be left here alone. I bet there's ghosts.'

'Don't be daft,' said Jack. 'Who needs ghosts when we've got her downstairs?'

'But I bet there is. I bet David thinks there is.'

They asked him. He hardly heard them because he had the sheet to his lips and was far away. Alec insisted. 'Are there any ghosts in this house, David?'

'I don't know,' he said, but the thought of the man on the landing drifted into his mind. He let it fade. It was too long ago and too misty, and he did not want the misery of that day to come back. 'I don't know.'

'You're hopeless you are. Anyway,' Alec turned over with a lot of noise, 'nothing would ever make me stay here by meself.'

'Nor me,' said Jack. 'Never.'

Christmas was a few days away and it brought an excitement that had nothing to do with parcels and presents. Christmas cards came from Newcastle with letters tucked inside from mothers saying that as there had been no raids for quite a while it was safe to come home for a short time. Everybody's cheeks seemed to be glowing with the same good news.

'And me Dad's on leave,' Jack shouted in the kitchen. 'Man, it's going to be great!'

Alec had a letter saying he was to catch the same bus as Jack, but David's letter was slow coming. It was the day before Christmas Eve, and Jack and Alec were already packed ready to leave that afternoon, when the post came with David's letter. They all crowded round to find out when he was leaving.

It was Pauline who told her mother what had happened. 'His little fingers were that clumsy he could hardly get it out of the envelope. Just like a baby he looks sometimes. And there was a letter and a postal order. "That'll be for your fare home," said one of the lads, but Davey was reading what his Mam said. I've never seen a look on a boy's face quite like I seen then. It was a lovely letter, I read it, but his Mam told him she didn't think it was safe and that he wasn't going to go home after all. I had to turn me back. The look in that little lad's eyes was something I never want to see again.'

David did not cry. Jack, watching him carefully, said, 'You're a good lad, Davey,' and then he and Alec whispered in the corner, and Pauline heard the chink of pennies. When they put on their coats and boots and went out secretively she knew that they were going down to the shop to buy him a present before their bus left. It was all they could do to cheer him up.

To prevent her own tears welling up again Pauline said, 'That's a pretty card your Mam sent, Davey. Nice little red robin.' He nodded. It was a tiny card, very small like his mother. 'But I don't believe you've sent one to her.'

'I did.'

'But not a proper one. Not one you made yourself. Anyone can send an old bought card.'

She knew he liked drawing. 'Tell you what,' she said as she led him to the window, 'see that old tree behind the yard? It's still got some lovely leaves on it, all red and yellow. Why don't you go and get some while I get a big piece of paper and make some flour paste, and then you can stick them on to your picture and send them to your Mam. There's still time; it's not Christmas Eve till tomorrow.'

She watched him cross the yard and then she smoothed her dress and bit her lips. His letter had been bad news for her, too, and the bell that suddenly rang meant that she had to face up to it.

Mrs Prosser's few Christmas cards were of the dark kind, and they stood among the black ornaments on the mantel as a reminder that Christmas was midwinter and cold and hard. Pauline felt their chill as she told Mrs Prosser that not all the boys were leaving for the holiday.

'Why's that? Has his mother no feeling?' The thin voice did not wait for an explanation. 'These people ought never to have children. They can't wait to saddle other people with them.' She waved Pauline away. 'Get the other two ready. I can't wait to see the back of them.'

Pauline fled. For the next hour there was bustle, and when Jack and Alec had given her David's present to hide, she went with them down to the village to make sure they caught the bus.

David was alone in the kitchen. All he could do now was to pretend. He pretended he was going home and he had to hurry to finish the big Christmas card he was making for his mother. He was drawing on the sheet of paper Pauline had given him when he heard the door to the hall open. He did not want to look up, but he slowly raised his eyes. Mrs Prosser stood there with her monkey fingers clasped in front of her black dress.

For a long moment neither moved, then her voice snapped at him, 'Stand up!' He slid off his chair. 'Stand up when a lady comes into the room!'

She swished forward so smoothly she seemed not to have legs under her long dress. 'So you're the one that's staying.' He saw her lips had bluish blisters. 'Your mother expects me to provide your Christmas dinner, I suppose. Oh does she, indeed!' Her breath hissed as she sucked it in. 'There will be no heathen feast in this house. No Christmas dinner, so don't expect it. The very idea!''

Indignation raged inside her, and she was turning away when quite suddenly she stopped. Her chin was pulled in so tightly it seemed to be part of her neck, and she was looking down at the table. 'What on earth is that?'

The red leaves were spread out in front of him, and for the first time David had a question he could answer. 'I'm going to stick them on a picture for me Mam.'

His voice was no more than a murmur, and her action was equally silent. She leant forward and scraped the leaves into one bony hand, crunched them like waste paper, and threw them into the back of the fire.

'That for your mother!' she said. 'I will not have my kitchen made into a Newcastle slum.' The door slammed.

When Pauline came back, David's picture was also on the fire. 'I didn't feel like doing it,' he said. He wanted to cry but he did not dare, and she did not question him.

She gave him all his favourite things for tea, and stayed with him late, reading a story to him as he lay in bed, something she had never done when the others were there.

When she tucked him in she whispered, 'I'll leave you the candle, Davey, but don't let on to the Missus.'

At the door she turned and smiled at him, then the latch dropped. He heard her footsteps on the stair, another door opened and closed, and he was in a silence so deep he thought he heard the flutter of the candle flame.

He lay as she had left him, curled up on his side, looking at Alec's empty bed. Behind him, Jack's bed would be the same—flat and empty. He was alone in the long room, and the frosty night crept in and held the candle flame stiff—as smooth as an almond. No sound, and all that emptiness at his back.

He turned his head on the pillow until he could see the wardrobe towering against the wall. From where he lay the long mirrors of its doors were blank, but the columns on either side shone in the candle flame as though they guarded a yawning gateway.

Then deep inside it something moved, and at the same instant a voice from almost alongside him dragged him round. The door to the stairs was open and the tall figure of Mrs Prosser was in the room. She made no noise. It was her reflection he had seen in the mirror.

'I knew it!' Her voice was as bitter as the icy air as she swept to the foot of his bed and pointed at the candle. 'Who gave you this?'

Words did not come. From his pillow he looked up at her. In the candlelight the blue flecks on her lips were black.

'Am I going to wait all night for an answer?'

The pointing hand suddenly clenched and he drew himself into a ball, ready for her to reach over and strike. But the blow did not come. Her hand came down, and something that may have been a smile pushed at her wrinkles. Even her voice was softer.

'But I don't suppose you like being on your own, do

you, sonny?' He shook his head. 'And I suppose you are afraid of the dark.' He nodded. 'Very, very afraid, I expect.'

He watched the wrinkles at the corner of her mouth deepen, and now she was definitely smiling. 'After all,' she said, 'it's almost Christmas.'

He tried to smile.

'Well,' she said, and her voice was still soft, 'you know you deserve a thrashing, don't you?' She waited for his nod. He had to give it. 'Worse than a thrashing in fact.' Her voice rose. 'And worse than a thrashing you shall have!'

As she spoke she snatched at the candle and turned for the door. 'You will stay in this room all night and all tomorrow until I tell you to come out!'

The flame streamed and dipped in front of her as she swept out. The door closed with a bang, and then the next, but even before he heard it slam he had scrabbled at the bedclothes and pulled them tight around himself as he crouched.

He heard himself sob, but the echo made the black room emptier and he stifled the sound. The sheets seemed clammy, as though they were never intended to be laid over a living creature, and his shivers made the iron bedstead give out little sounds like beetles' feet until he clamped his arms around his knees and controlled the trembling.

He heard a night bird shriek briefly on the hillside above the house, and then it, too, was swallowed in the silence of the night and everything was utterly still. He could not hear even the sound of his own breathing, but as his eyes stared into the darkness, and the silence in the room became more dense, he gradually saw the shape of the window against the stars.

It was then, in the corner beyond the foot of the bed, that he heard something shift. His bones were rigid, as cold as iron. He was clamped motionless.

Silence. His breath crept into his mouth. Then the sound came again. His eyes were as wide as an owl's, and in the starlight he saw the wardrobe door sigh open.

He flung himself across the empty bed, and his feet were on cold lino as his fingers fumbled for the latch. It bit his fingers, but the door was open and he plunged into the blackness of the stairs. His foot missed the tread. He clutched for the handrail but missed it and fell, twisting in the rushing darkness until his shoulder and back crashed into the door at the bottom. The catch burst and he fell out on to the bare boards of the landing.

There was a glimmer of light downstairs. Mrs Prosser had stopped and was looking up. Her face halted him. The candle, gleaming like a star, made her mouth a pitiless shadow and her eyes two dark pits. But he had to go down to escape from whatever had swung the wardrobe door. He was too late. Something large and dark moved out from the burst doorway and brushed past him. He could see it against the whitewashed wall; the shape of a man, blocking his way.

David shrank. He was no more than a fistful of fear, and the man looked down at him. In the faint light from below, the man's face was hardly visible. It was no more than a blur of heavy moustache and eyebrows, which threw a deep shadow over its eyes, but David felt their gaze and his blood slowed, and the silence stiffened until it seemed nothing would move again.

It was then that the figure turned away. He watched it as it began to descend, seeming to tread heavily, but no sound came. The well of the stairs was a column of silence, with the spark of the candle shining faintly. Mrs Prosser's head was still tilted upwards. She saw what was coming, and the candle trembled, but she did not move. Fear held her motionless until it was too late.

The figure of the man was only two steps above her

when, in a sudden stab of terror, she thrust the candle at him as though to scorch him out of the air. But his big hand reached and closed over hers. It was then that she cried out and began to struggle. She could not save herself. The candle flared, fell and went out.

As darkness engulfed the whole staircase, David ran down into it, sliding his hand down the banister. Nothing would keep him alone at the top of the house. He heard Mrs Prosser fall. She did not cry out or even moan. He heard the thud of her arms, hips and head on the stairs, a soft slither, then silence.

He remembered the sole of his foot treading on something warm that yielded beneath it, but then he was over it and crossing the cold floor of the kitchen to the back door.

His mother came that day, not to fetch him but to stay that night and the next, over Christmas. They were in Pauline's house down in the village with the stream outside the door, where she had found him standing on the ice.

'I don't know how we are ever going to thank you,' said his mother for the tenth time. She was still shy, sitting very upright in the easy chair by the big fire as Pauline bustled about fetching tea. 'It was such a terrible shock when I got your message.'

Pauline's mother, round-cheeked like her daughter, smiled. 'Now just you put your mind at rest. Davey stays with us from now on. He could hardly go back there, could he?'

The two women looked at each other. They understood one another. David, in the warmth of the fire with the tinsel of the Christmas tree trembling at his elbow, bowed his head over the drawing pad on his knee and pretended he was not listening as all three lowered their voices.

'Poor soul. What a terrible way to go.'

'And that little lad in the house all on his own. He hasn't said much about it, and I don't like to ask.'

Pauline glanced at him, and he started to hum to himself and bent further over his drawing. She turned her back to him and lowered her voice even further. 'She must have been up in his room. Must have been. I'm just sure one of those boys told her what was up there, because she had it with her when we found her at the foot of the stairs. It must have been the last thing she saw before she died.'

David's mother did not understand.

'Mr Prosser's old suit,' said Pauline. 'It was wrapped around her. Tight. Really tight.'

David's picture had a house standing in the snow, and you could see firelight through the windows. He would give it to his mother in the morning.

Mandy Kiss Mommy

LANCE SALWAY

The present arrived on a Saturday morning. I know it was Saturday because we were all having breakfast together in the kitchen when the doorbell rang. If it had been a weekday, we wouldn't have been sitting down at all. Not at the same time, that is. Breakfast on weekdays usually meant cereal and toast gulped on the run as we hunted for lost gym shoes and last night's homework. Mother didn't eat at all on weekday mornings, and Dad always left the house at seven, long before the rest of us got up. On Saturdays, though, we all sat down to breakfast together. And that's why I remember that the present arrived on a Saturday morning. The morning of Mandy's tenth birthday.

When the doorbell rang, Mandy jumped to her feet. 'That'll be the postman,' she said. 'I'll go.'

As she disappeared into the hall, my parents smiled at each other. 'Not more presents, surely!' Dad said.

I could see what he meant. The kitchen table was already littered with torn wrapping paper and birthday cards, and books and records, and the shapeless knitted garments that our grandmother always sent on special occasions. I'd given Mandy some money, as this was the kind of present that she liked more than anything else. I hadn't given her *much*, of course, because I didn't *have* much to give, but even a pound was better than nothing. Mandy was a miser. She collected money in the way that other people collect stamps and matchbox labels. She also collected dead beetles.

My mother stood up. 'Come on, Jennifer,' she said. 'Help me clear the table, will you?'

But Mandy ran back into the kitchen then and we turned towards her instead. She was carrying a large brown paper parcel, and her eyes were shining with excitement. 'It's come!' she said. 'Abigail's present. I knew she wouldn't forget. I *knew* it!'

My mother sat down again. 'No,' she said in a voice as cold as stone. 'No, Abigail never forgets.'

There was an awkward silence then, for we all knew that my mother didn't like Abigail. But one could hardly blame her; Abigail had once been married to my father.

It happened a long time ago, of course. Before I was born. My father and Abigail had met when they were students at university. He had been swept off his feet, or so he said, because she was dark, amusing and American. Dad was shy, clever, and very English, so they couldn't have been more different in character. Perhaps this was why their marriage had lasted only two years. Abigail went back to Massachusetts when she found out that Dad wanted to marry my mother, and that should have been the end of the story. But Abigail and Dad stayed in touch and, when I was born, and when Mandy followed three years later, she began to send us presents at Christmas and on our birthdays. Dad often said that Abigail looked on us as her own family, but my mother always laughed scornfully at this and said that Abigail should have children of her own if she wanted them so badly; she had no business inflicting herself on us.

But Abigail didn't inflict herself on us. We had never even seen her. I think that she and my mother did meet once when Abigail came to England on a sabbatical, but my mother wouldn't talk about it, and I don't think that they got on very well. All that Mandy and I knew of Abigail were the large, mysterious parcels which arrived promptly on our birthdays postmarked Salem, Mass.

Abigail's presents were always exciting and always unusual. She once sent me a length of Indian silk, embroidered with tiny mirrors, and an elephant carved from jade. Then came an enormous Chinese kite in the shape of a fish, together with a Roman coin and a straw hat from Tahiti fringed with seashells. Whenever a parcel arrived, we would watch in wonder as each extraordinary object emerged from its shell of brown paper like an exotic butterfly shedding a chrysalis. One Christmas she sent a box of old Valentine cards decorated with embossed golden cupids, and lace, and beads, and artificial flowers. My last birthday parcel contained an ostrich-feather fan and an Egyptian clockwork monkey that played the banjo. Once, she'd sent a genuine shrunken head from Ecuador. The gifts were strange and beautiful, like Abigail herself, but they made me uneasy. They seemed out of place in our ordinary house, like orchids blooming in a cabbage patch. And there was an air of menace about the gifts that I couldn't explain. They seemed, somehow, venomous.

Only my mother appeared to share my misgivings, but I think she disliked the gifts for quite different reasons. She would turn away from them with an angry frown and a dismissive wave of her hand. 'Why does Abigail waste her money year after year?' she would say bitterly. 'Why can't she leave us alone?'

Then Dad would laugh nervously and say, 'What does it matter? She's only trying to be kind. And anyway, she can afford it. Her family owns half Massachusetts.'

And my mother would snort and look unconvinced.

Now she started to clear the table as Mandy opened her parcel.

'Here, let me, Mandy,' Dad said after a while. 'You're all fingers and thumbs.'

'I wonder what it'll be this time!' said Mandy. She was trembling with excitement.

'More foreign rubbish, I expect,' my mother muttered from the larder.

Mandy and I watched in silence as Dad removed the last of the wrapping paper to reveal a large cardboard box.

'You take over now, Mandy,' he said. 'It's your present, after all.' He pushed the box towards her.

Mandy opened the box carefully and peered inside. We all watched her, waiting for the smile of wonder and delight that we had come to expect. But this time Mandy didn't smile. Instead, her mouth fell open with astonishment.

'What is it?' I asked urgently. 'What *is* it?'

Mandy's voice was flat with disappointment. 'It's a doll. She's sent me a stupid old ordinary doll.'

'She can't have. Let me see.'

Mandy was right. There *was* a doll inside. But it wasn't like those that Abigail had sent in the past: antique Victorian dolls with fragile china faces and elaborate lace underwear, or sinister old-lady dolls made from dried apples. This was a large moon-faced doll with shiny black hair, and eyes that opened and shut, and a red cupid's-bow mouth, and a frilly pink dress. There was a label tied to one of the plump plastic hands which read: *'Hi! My name is Mandy. Will you be my mommy?'*

I couldn't believe my eyes. We stared at the doll in horrified silence until my mother, puzzled by our reaction, came across to look.

'I don't *believe* it!' she said. 'Isn't it *awful*! I've never seen anything quite so hideous in my life.' And she began to laugh, a shrill laugh of sheer delight.

'It's not funny!' Mandy said miserably. 'She's sent me a *doll*. I'm too old for dolls. It's horrible. I hate it! I hate it!'

My mother stopped laughing and said, 'Perhaps it's a joke. Abigail can't be serious, surely? Her presents are usually so—so *pretentious*. And this doll is—well, it's rubbish, isn't it?'

'Oh, I don't know,' Dad muttered loyally. 'It's not as bad as all that.'

'But it *is*,' my mother insisted. 'We'll just have to give it away.'

Mandy looked at her sharply. 'What do you mean?'

'We'll give it away,' my mother explained. 'To a jumble sale. Or Oxfam. *Someone* may like it. Although,' and she gave a harsh laugh, 'I can't imagine who.'

'No!' Mandy shouted. 'No, you can't!'

We were all taken aback by her sudden anger.

'What do you mean, dear?' my mother asked after a pause. 'You said that you don't like the doll.'

'But it's *mine*,' Mandy said fiercely. 'It's *my* doll. *You* can't give it away. It's mine. She belongs to *me*.'

'Her name's Mandy, too,' I pointed out. 'It says so on the label. And she's got black hair just like yours.'

My mother peered at the label. 'Really, how absurd! "Will you be my mommy?" But then it *is* American, after all.'

'Of course it's American,' said my father irritably. 'Abigail's American. What do you expect?'

'I expect a little more taste,' my mother said frostily. Then she turned away. 'Do what you like with the thing. I couldn't care less. As long as I don't have to set eyes on it again.'

There was an awkward silence. Then Mandy lifted the doll out of the box. She stared into the bright black eyes for a moment and then she smiled. 'My name's Mandy, too,' she whispered. And she cradled the doll in her arms.

'Look,' I said. 'What's that?'

'What do you mean?' Mandy asked.

'There's something hanging from the doll's back. It looks like a piece of string.'

'Pull it and see what happens,' Dad suggested. 'It's probably some sort of mechanical device.'

Mandy pulled the short cord which hung from the back of the doll's pink frilly dress. There was a pause and then a loud tinny voice sounded from somewhere deep inside the doll, a voice which said over and over again: 'Mandy kiss Mommy. Mandy kiss Mommy. Mandy kiss Mommy.'

We listened in fascinated horror until the voice died away. I didn't know whether to laugh or cry.

It was my mother who broke the silence. 'Well, *really!*' she snorted. 'Have you ever seen anything more *vulgar*? The sooner you get rid of it, the better, Mandy.'

'No,' Mandy said. 'I won't. She's mine. She's my present. And *you* can leave it alone.'

'Don't you talk to *me* like that, young lady,' my mother said firmly. 'Any more of it and you'll go straight to your room, birthday or no birthday.'

'Don't worry,' Mandy said, in a voice as sharp as steel. 'I'm going anyway. With my present. My present from Abigail.'

And she turned and stalked out of the kitchen, leaving the rest of us open-mouthed behind her.

In the days that followed, Mandy refused to be parted from the doll. She didn't take it with her to school, of course, but the two of them seemed inseparable once she returned home. I would sometimes come across them sitting in silence on the landing or in a corner of the garden, and when I did I often felt that I had interrupted a private conversation. Mandy had always been a friendly child, and the house was usually thronged with her noisy friends, but one by one they stopped coming. Now Mandy seemed content to be alone with the doll. And the only sound we heard from her room was the monotonous metallic whine: 'Mandy kiss Mommy. Mandy kiss Mommy. Mandy kiss Mommy.'

'Why don't you ask some friends over for tea tomorrow?' my mother suggested to Mandy one morning. 'Janey, and Kate, and Rachel Thingummy. And that Robinson child. Veronica? Victoria? Virginia?'

'Viola,' said Mandy.

'Well, whatever her name is, ask her over. I'll make a cake.'

'I don't want to,' Mandy said. 'I don't want them. I don't *like* them.'

There was a pause. Then, 'Why not?' my mother asked quietly.

Mandy looked at her. 'My doll doesn't like them. She doesn't like them at all.' And she reached out for the doll and once again the nasty tinny voice rang round the kitchen: 'Mandy kiss Mommy. Mandy kiss Mommy. Mandy kiss . . .'

'Get that thing out of here!' my mother shouted. 'If you don't, *I* will!'

'Don't you touch it!' Mandy snapped, and ran from the room.

When she had gone, my mother sighed loudly and said, 'I don't know what's got into that child, I really don't. All she does is moon about with that stupid doll. One of these days I'll . . .' She caught my eye then and stopped. 'Well, I'll do *something*,' she went on lamely. 'One of these days.'

That night I overheard my parents arguing about Mandy when I passed their door on my way to the bathroom.

'It's unhealthy,' my mother was saying. 'She spends all her time with that wretched thing. It's like—like having another *person* in the house.'

'Oh, don't exaggerate,' Dad said wearily.

'It's all very well for you. You're hardly ever here. I'm the one who has to cope with her. She's changed, you know. She's a different child. Her teacher says so, too.'

My mother lowered her voice then. 'Do you know, I sometimes think she talks to that doll.'

'Of course she does,' Dad sighed. 'All little girls talk to their dolls.'

'Mandy's not a little girl,' my mother snapped. '*And* she's big for her age. Besides, that's no ordinary doll. Sometimes I think . . .'

'What?'

'Well, sometimes I think Mandy's *possessed* by it. Haunted.'

Dad started to laugh. 'You're mad,' he chuckled. 'Nutty as a fruitcake.'

My mother began to sound desperate then. 'I tell you I can't take much more. And if I hear that voice again, I don't know what I'll do.' She raised her voice in a poor imitation of the doll's whine. '"Mandy kiss Mommy. Mandy kiss Mommy. . . ."' Then, 'I'll give her "Mandy kiss Mommy." And as for Abigail . . . It's all her fault. Her and her fancy presents. Why does she do it? Why?'

'For God's sake keep your voice down,' my father whispered. 'Jennifer's still awake. She'll hear.'

Their voices dropped then and I couldn't make out any more. When I came back from the bathroom, I passed Mandy's room. The door was open, and I peered in. She was fast asleep. Beside her bed, on a chair, stood the doll. Abigail's doll. I stared at it, entranced by the shiny hair and the bright smile and the dark eyes that glittered in the half-light and seemed to gaze straight into mine. And, as I watched, I could have sworn—but no, it was just my imagination. Surely I only imagined that the doll's bright red mouth twisted open in a mocking smile . . .

Nothing was the same after that. Each day, when she came home from school, Mandy went straight to her room and stayed there. My mother bustled about as usual and pretended that nothing was wrong, but I'm sure that she, like me, was picturing Mandy in her room with the doll and that she, too, was imagining the gleaming black hair and the pink plastic face and the tinny chant of 'Mandy kiss Mommy'.

And then, about a week later, when my mother and I were getting tea ready, Mandy stormed into the kitchen and slammed the door behind her.

'What on earth . . .' my mother began.

'Where is she?' Mandy shouted, her face distorted with rage. 'What have you done with the doll?'

My mother looked at her calmly and said, 'I don't know what you mean. And if you don't stop shouting, I'll send you straight back to your room. I won't tolerate . . .'

'*Where is she?*' Mandy screamed.

'What's happened?' I asked.

Mandy turned to me. 'My doll has gone,' she said. 'I can't find her anywhere. I've looked.' Then she turned back to my mother. '*You've* taken her, haven't you? You never liked her. You hate her. You said so. Yes, you hate her. And you hate *me*.' She sat down and started to cry.

My mother waited for a moment, listening to the harsh sobs and trying to control her temper. Then, 'Go to your room, Mandy,' she said quietly. 'This nonsense has got to stop. I haven't got your doll. I don't know where it is.'

Mandy stood up. When she spoke, her voice was harsh and bitter with hate. 'You took the doll,' she said. 'I know you did. And I'll never forgive you. Never.'

Later that evening, when I was in my room trying to learn irregular French verbs, there was a knock at the door.

'Go away whoever you are,' I said irritably, but the door opened and Mandy came in. She had a triumphant grin on her face, and she was carrying the doll.

'I've found her,' she said.

'So I see. Where was she?'

Mandy's face hardened. 'In the dustbin. Right at the bottom, underneath all the—all the rubbish. Where *she* put her.'

She thrust the doll at me and I turned my face away. I didn't want to touch it again. I didn't want to see the glittering dark eyes, the mouth . . .

'She's all grubby,' Mandy said calmly, 'but I can clean her up. I can mend the tear in her dress. But I don't know what to do about the voice.'

I looked at her then. 'What do you mean?'

'The voice is broken,' Mandy said. 'She's broken the voice. Listen.'

She pulled the cord on the doll's back. There was silence at first and then a whirring noise and after that the familiar metallic tones that I hated so much. But the words were different now, jumbled:

'Mandy Mandy kiss Mandy Mommy kiss Mommy kiss Mommy Mandy kill Mandy kill Mommy kill Mommy Mandy kill Mommy Mandy kill Mommy . . .'

'Do you hear what she's saying?' Mandy whispered. 'Do you hear it, Jennifer?'

Yes, I could hear. But I didn't believe it. I couldn't believe it.

'The machine's broken,' I said, as the voice died away. 'It's a mistake. Dad'll mend it. When he gets back.' My father had gone away to a conference in Leeds.

'Yes,' Mandy said calmly. She looked at me steadily with her cold dark eyes. 'She shouldn't have done it, should she? She shouldn't have taken the doll.'

'Don't be stupid!' I shouted as she walked to the door. 'Come back, Mandy. I want to tell you . . .'

But she didn't come back. I stared at the door, not wanting to believe what I'd heard, not wanting to re-member. But I couldn't forget the hatred in Mandy's eyes. And I couldn't forget the doll's blank stare and the whining, whirring voice.

I couldn't sleep that night. Whenever I closed my eyes, the doll's pale face swam into my mind, the dark eyes mocking me, daring me. And, try as I might, I couldn't shut out the sound of that hideous metallic voice chanting those awful words. And I saw my sister's face, too, clenched with hate. And my mother's, shocked, bewildered, and angry. And I felt terribly afraid.

I suppose I must have fallen asleep, because the next thing I remember is waking with a start. I felt sure that a sudden noise had woken me for my heart was pounding. I sat up and listened, but I could hear nothing. I lay down again, but the fear remained and I couldn't sleep. I stared into the darkness, listening, remembering, and then I got up and opened my bedroom door. There was a light shining under Mandy's door, and I crept up to it and listened. I could hear the murmur of voices, one soft and gentle, the other sharp and strident.

I turned the handle and went inside. Mandy was sitting on the bed, cradling the doll in her arms. She turned her pale face towards me as I came in.

'Mandy,' I began, 'there's something I have to . . .'

I stopped when I heard the voice, the awful voice of the doll. 'Mandy kiss Mommy. Mandy kiss Mommy. Mandy kiss Mommy. Mandy kiss . . .'

Mandy looked at me questioningly. 'What is it, Jennifer?' she asked. 'Can't you sleep?'

'No,' I said. 'Listen, Mandy, I . . .' Then I stopped. Something was different. The doll was different. Something about the voice . . . 'The doll!' I said excitedly. 'The words have changed. She's not saying . . .'

'Yes,' said Mandy. 'She doesn't need to say it now.'

I didn't understand what she meant at first. There was something more important on my mind. Something I had to tell Mandy.

'It was me,' I said quickly. 'I did it. I'm sorry.'

My sister's gaze was expressionless. 'What do you mean?'

'I hid the doll in the dustbin. I—I must have broken the voice. It was me. I'm sorry.'

I stared at the floor in the silence that followed. I didn't dare look at the doll.

'It doesn't matter,' Mandy said at last. 'The doll is back now. And the voice isn't broken. That's all that matters.'

I stared at her in disbelief. She was so calm. She wasn't angry at all. 'Did you hear what I said? *I* took the doll. It's all my fault. I'm . . .' And then I remembered Mandy's earlier words. 'What did you mean?' I asked.

'What did you mean?' I repeated. 'You said that the doll doesn't need to say it now.'

Mandy smiled then, a twisted, mocking smile. And her eyes were dark and cold.

'What did you mean?' I shouted. '*Tell me!*'

Then I saw the blood. The blood on the doll. On the doll's hands and on the dress. And I knew what she meant. I knew exactly what she meant. But I didn't start to scream until I reached my mother's bedroom and opened the door.

A Kind of Swan Song

HELEN CRESSWELL

When I say that Lisa was someone special, right from the beginning, I expect that you will smile. *All* mothers think their children are special—and so they are, of course. In my case, Lisa was my only child, and so you will think that perhaps it is only natural that I should think her special. And when I tell you that my husband (who was a violinist with a well-known symphony orchestra) died when she was only a few months old, then you will quite understandably suspect me of exaggeration. I don't blame you. This is how it might seem.

But I must insist—Lisa *was* special. And perhaps it is partly because it is important to me that other people should realize this too, that I am now writing her story. It will not take long. She was only eight when she died.

The other reason I feel bound to tell her story is because I want you to know, as certainly as I now do myself, that death is not the end, not a full stop.

'Ah,' I hear you say, 'but she is *bound* to say that. She had no one in the world but her little daughter, and she died. Now she is trying to convince herself that death is not the end of everything. It's understandable, but she can't expect *us* to believe that!'

To this I simply reply—'Wait. Wait until you have heard my story. Then decide.'

At birth, Lisa was special to Peter and myself in exactly the same way as any other baby born to loving parents.

In our case, there was an extra dimension to our joy, because we knew already that in Peter's case it was to be short-lived. We knew that he had only a few months, at most, to savour the delights of parenthood. He had had to leave the orchestra several weeks before her birth. And so, for those first few months of Lisa's life Peter was as close to her as any father can be: He would sit with her for hours, studying her tiny, peaceful face as if he wanted to imprint it on his heart forever. In the early days, before he grew too weak, he would bathe her, change her, put her to bed.

And then he would play music to her, for hours on end. Not himself—he had sorrowfully put his violin away before her birth, but on tapes, and records. She would lie there kicking on the rug to the strains of Bach and Mozart, songs of Schubert and grand opera.

Sometimes I would laugh and say that I thought it all rather beyond the grasp of a baby, and that we should be playing her nursery rhymes instead. But he would say, quite seriously, 'That baby may not be able to talk, yet, but she can hear. She is listening, the whole time, trying to make a pattern of this strange new world she has entered. If what she hears is joyful, if she hears harmony, then all her life long she will seek out joy and harmony for herself. Believe me, Martha, I know that I am right.'

Even at the time I acknowledged that what he said might be true. Now, I know that it was.

I don't want to give the impression by this that we were too serious about things, or that Lisa had a strange start in life. Like any young parents we romped and played with her, looked for ways of making her smile or, better still, laugh. And we sang nursery rhymes as well. But I honestly think that the times she loved best, the times when she seemed happiest, were when she was lying there listening to music—especially songs. There was a special peaceful, wondering look she seemed to wear when she heard a beautiful human voice singing great music.

I don't want to exaggerate this—it is how I remember it, but then perhaps my memory of that time is not very reliable. It is a strange thing for a woman to watch her child blossom and at the same time her husband, the father, fading. Joy and sorrow could hardly be more poignantly interwoven.

Peter refused to let me grieve openly, and himself would show no sign of bitterness that he must soon leave us.

'I want there to be no shadows over her,' he said. 'Let her be shaped by music, not by sorrow.'

Strangely, afterwards, when she was four or five, she would insist that she remembered Peter, though she could not really have done so.

'He was always smiling,' she would say. And that was certainly true, so far as she was concerned. If there were times when he allowed his smile to fade, it was never in her presence.

He died when she was just over eight months old—in time to see her crawling, but before she took her first steps.

'Promise you will keep playing her music,' he said before he died. And of course I promised. And that was another strange thing.

In those unreal, nightmarish days after he died, Lisa grew pale and quiet. It was as if she, too, were mourning. Then, coming back into the house after the funeral, drained and weary, I was suddenly aware of the great silence and absence. It occurred to me that since Peter died, I had played no music. I went and put on a record—one of his favourites, from Haydn's 'Creation'. As the pure, triumphant notes swelled about me, I lay back in a chair and surrendered myself to it. Then, beyond that marvellous music, I heard, in a pause, another music, another voice—Lisa's.

I hurried into the next room where she lay, as I thought, sleeping. Instead, she lay there wide eyed—and round mouthed, too. Her whole tiny being seemed intent on the sounds that she was making with such seriousness, such concentration—Lisa was singing.

Very well—perhaps she was not. Perhaps she was simply cooing, crooning, as babies do. But to me, in my overwrought condition, it seemed that she was singing, herself joining in Haydn's great celebratory hymn. I remember that my tears, all at once released, splashed down onto her face, and that I gathered her up and took her with me, and she lay against me while we listened together.

Some children walk before they talk, some the other way round. Lisa, I swear, sang before she did either. I have the courage to say this, in the light of what came after. I did not merely imagine that Lisa was a child of music. She quite simply, and unarguably, was.

At first it was only I who knew it, and who could hardly believe it when I heard that infant voice playing with scales as other children play with bricks. (She did that, too. She was in every way exactly like all other children of her age. Only this was different—music ran in her veins.)

Then, as she grew older and we went to playgroups, others would remark on the purity and the pitch of her voice, and noticed that she had only to hear a song once to know it off by heart.

'She takes after her father,' they all said.

It was true. But only I knew that she was composing music, as well as singing it. She would lie in bed after I had tucked her in for the night, her voice tracing its own melodies in the darkness. Sometimes even I, her own mother, would give a little shiver.

The word 'genius' is not an easy one to come to terms with. Every mother, as I have said, believes her own child to be special. But I do not think that any mother is looking for genius. It is rather a frightening thing, for ordinary people. We admit that it exists—but at a great distance, and in other people (preferably long since dead!).

At two Lisa was picking out tunes on the piano; at three she was playing both piano and violin. But it was the singing that mattered, I knew that. I watched her grow and develop with a delight tinged with sadness. I knew even then that the days of our closeness were numbered. Soon the world would discover her, and then the music would no longer be our shared secret.

When she was only four photographs of her were beginning to appear in the papers, under headlines such as 'Child Prodigy wins Premier Award at Festival' and 'Little Lisa Triumphs Again.'

I don't want you to think that she was in any way strange. She was exactly like every other little girl in most ways. She loved reading, roller-skating and using her computer. When she started school, her marks were average. It was only the music that set her apart.

When she was five all kinds of renowned people—professors and teachers of music—began to visit us.

'Soon,' I thought, 'they will take her away from me.'

They wanted me, even then, to send her away to a special school, where her gift could be nurtured.

'It doesn't need nurturing,' I told them. 'It is natural. It will flower of its own accord.'

They went away again, but I knew that it would not be for long. I knew, too that what I had told them was only partly true. *Any* gift needs the right nourishment, just as a rare and fragile plant.

Lisa herself began to grow away from me. Not in the things that mattered—the things between mother and daughter. In those things we were always close. We teased each other a lot, and sometimes, even then, it would seem as if she were older than I was.

'Dear goose mother!' she would say, if I forgot something, or made a mistake. It became her pet name for me.

At six they tried to take her away again, and again I resisted.

'It's too soon,' I said. 'She's too young. Leave her with me a little longer, then she can go.'

This time, when they had gone, I thought I could sense a sadness in her, a disappointment. I thought perhaps that I was being selfish, over-possessive. And so when they came again, begging me, almost, to send her away, I gave in.

Her delight when she heard the news hurt me, and she must have seen this.

'I'll still be home in the holidays, dear goose mother,' she told me. 'Don't be sad, or you'll spoil it for me.'

So I tried to look glad, for her sake. During those last few months together before she went away, I gathered her music together, to comfort me in her absence. Every song she composed I made her sing into a microphone so that I could record it. I recorded her playing the piano and the violin too, but it was the singing that mattered. We both knew that. When she sang, instrument and music were one, perfect and inviolable.

She was still only seven when she left for her new school. She was radiant. She was like a bride in beret and navy socks.

'No crying, goose mother,' she told me. 'We'll write to each other.'

'And send me tapes,' I said. 'Please, Lisa. Don't let even a single song you make get away. Put it on tape. That way, we've got it forever.'

She smiled then with a curious wisdom.

'It's *making* the song that matters,' she said. 'Nothing gets away—ever.'

When she had gone, I *did* cry, as I knew I would, and I kept remembering those words. How could she *know*, I wondered, something that most people never learn in a lifetime?

I took a job—an interesting one, really—in a house belonging to the National Trust, and open to visitors. Even so, that first term dragged. Most evenings I would sit and listen to the tapes we had made that summer. And at weekends I'd go shopping—looking for little things to put in her stocking. Lisa still believed (at least, I think she did) in Father Christmas.

By mid-December she was home. For a day or so we were a little strange together, and then it was as though she had never been away. One evening, we turned on the television to see a programme of carols composed by children. It was a competition, and these were the winning entries. When it was over, Lisa said quietly,

'Next year, goose mother, *I* shall make a carol!'

That was all. It was so slight a thing that, were it not for what followed, I doubt whether I should have remembered it. Lisa, after all, had been making songs almost all her life. What was more natural than that she should make a carol?

Christmas and the New Year came and went. This time, when she left for school, the wrench was not so painful. We can become in time accustomed to most things—even to the absence of those we love. It all seemed inevitable, and for me, it was also part of the promise I had made to Peter before he died.

Lisa's letters came every week—badly spelt, and full of the things she was doing, the music she was making. They were full, too, of the ordinary things—requests for clothes that were all the rage, for stamps to swap and posters for her room. That term passed, and the next. In the summer I took a cottage in the Lakes, and we spent most of the time walking and cycling. We were well on the way to establishing a pattern to our lives.

It was sometimes hard to remember that she was still only eight-years-old. And we never talked about what she would 'do' when she was 'grown up'. Looking back, I think that this was because she was already what she was meant to be. She was all the time in a process of becoming, and this was all that was necessary. She knew it herself.

'It's *making* the song that matters,' she had said, over a year ago.

Again I waved her off to the start of a new school year. This time the ache was not so bad. I even registered for evening classes in Italian, and went out occasionally with friends to the theatre, or for a meal. But Lisa still made the tapes, and I still played them, hour upon hour. Now, she was beginning to write her own words to the music. One day I received a cassette with a song called 'Goose Mother' and I felt so happy and so honoured that I actually taped it again, onto another cassette, for fear that it might get lost or damaged. Even as I did so, I seemed to hear her saying, 'It's *making* the song that matters'. I smiled wryly.

'For you, perhaps,' I thought. 'But for the rest of us, who can only listen, it's the song itself that counts.'

In November I was surprised by Lisa calling me on the telephone. This she had done only once before—to inform me that she had chicken pox, but there was no need to worry, and proudly announce the number of spots she had.

'Listen,' she said, 'I've made a carol!'

'A carol?' I echoed.

'Remember—that competition we saw? And listen—Davey's going home, for the weekend, and I can go with him! So you and I can record it together—on our own piano!'

'Darling, that's wonderful!' I said. 'But . . .'

'Look—his mother's coming to fetch us in the car. I'll be home Friday, at around six. Can't stop now—bye!'

That was all. It was Tuesday—three days to get used to the wonderful fact that Lisa was coming home. I had quite forgotten (how could I?) that during their first year children at the school were not allowed to go home during termtime, but that this rule was lifted after that.

I spent the interim pleasurably shopping for Lisa's favourite food (not a difficult task, this being mainly a variation on chicken) and bought a new duvet cover for her bedroom. By half-past-five on the Friday I was fidgeting in the kitchen—opening and re-opening the oven door to check on the degree of brownness of chicken and potatoes, wondering whether I should start thawing the chocolate mousse.

At quarter-to-six I remembered that I hadn't any fizzy lemonade—her favourite drink, and one not allowed at school. I hesitated.

'I'll write a note,' I thought, 'and pin it on the door. I'll only be five minutes.'

Accordingly I wrote 'Back in five minutes' and pinned it on the door and set off. There were no shops nearby. I took the car and made for the nearest late-night supermarket. The traffic was dense, irritatingly slow. I had forgotten what Friday night rush hours were like. At one point, I almost seized the opportunity to turn round and go home without the lemonade. But, I reflected, people rarely arrived on time, especially at the weekends. I carried on.

It was nearly quarter-past-six when I arrived back. In the space my own car had occupied only half-an-hour previously, was another. It was a police car. I drew alongside it, oblivious to the hooting behind me. Two figures, a policeman and a policewoman were standing on the steps up to the front door.

I wrenched open the door and got out. I was telling myself to keep calm. My knees were trembling.

'What—what is it?'

They turned. Their faces were young, worried, pitying.

'Mrs Viner?'

I nodded.

'Perhaps we can . . . ?'

I hardly remember what happened then exactly. Somehow I was inside, somehow I was sitting in my usual chair facing the fire and a voice was talking to me. It was a sympathetic voice, its owner reluctant to give me the news. 'Motorway . . . wet surface . . . central reservation . . . lorry . . .' The words washed over me. What they were telling me was that Lisa was dead. She had been killed, along with her friend and his mother, on the motorway.

They were very kind. The young woman made me a cup of tea and switched off the oven. Before they left they stood looking at me uncertainly, at a loss. They didn't know what to say.

'Funny thing,' said the policeman, 'we'd been there on the steps ten minutes before you came.'

I said nothing.

'Could've sworn there was someone in here,' he went on. 'Could hear someone singing—a kid, it sounded like.'

'We wondered if the radio had been left on,' the girl added.

'And now I come to think of it,' he said, 'the radio *wasn't* on. Or the telly. Funny, that. . . .'

'Yes, funny.' I said. 'Thank you. Thank you both very much. I think—I think I want to be alone now.'

They hesitated.

'Sure you'll be all right?'

'Sure.'

They went. The door closed and I was alone. I sat there for I don't know how long. I was seeing Lisa, hearing her, trying to tell myself that I would never see or hear her again. I couldn't cry. I just sat, dry-eyed, remembering.

In the end, after a long dark age, I got up. Mechanically I began turning things off, locking up for the night. The front door, the back, check the oven—still containing the chicken and crisp potatoes—switch off lights, pull out the plug of the TV. . . .

I stopped. All the lights but one were out. There, glowing in the darkness, were the red and green lights of the stereo deck and cassette recorder. There was a very faint hum. My mind was dense, confused. I had set *up* the system, that very afternoon, all ready to record the carol. The blank cassette was in place, I had carefully checked the sound levels. *And then I had switched it off.*

I remembered doing it. I had actually thought of the way Peter had always chided me for leaving things on—especially the cassette recorder. He had lectured me about the damage it might do.

I advanced towards the deck. Hesitantly, I pressed the PLAY switch. There came only a faint hissing. Then, hardly knowing why I did so, I pressed REWIND. *The tape rewound.* It stopped with a click.

'But it was a new cassette,' I thought. 'Brand new.'

I stood there for a long time in the dim remaining light. Then I pressed another key—PLAY.

The room filled with sound. A voice—Lisa's voice, pure and sweet, sang:

On a far midnight,

Long, long ago. . . .

There was no accompaniment, no piano, just that young, miraculous voice, singing of that long-ago miracle that Christmas celebrates.

I stood dazed, listening. Then, when at last the carol

ended, I heard—or thought I heard (it certainly was not there on the tape, afterwards)—'There, dear goose mother! I told you—it's *making* the song that matters!'

And I knew that this was her last present to me. It was not for her own sake, but for mine, that the carol was there, locked for all time, on tape.

I sent that tape to the contest. It won. The presenter said, 'It is with great sadness that we have to tell you that Lisa, aged eight, died tragically in a car accident, just after she had recorded this carol for our contest. It was to be her swan song.'

Only I knew that the carol had been recorded not before, but after the accident. Though perhaps it could, after all, be called a *kind* of swan song.

Ivor

GEORGE MACKAY BROWN

Ten years ago, my mother rented a house in Hamnavoe in the Orkneys for the whole summer. My mother was a serious archaeologist; there were plenty of ancient monuments for her to explore. And there was a 'dig' on that summer, a thousand-year-old Viking farm.

(My parents were divorced. My father doesn't come into this story.)

North we went, by train and ferryboat, my mother, three sisters older than me, and my frightened sea-sick self. The ferry-boat, *St Ola*, passed under the immense red cliffs of Hoy, the highest perpendicular cliffs in Britain.

The house we were to live in was built on a stone jetty, or pier, that jutted into the harbour of the little port—an old eighteenth-century stone house of three storeys.

We shared the pier with an old couple who lived in another house. The old man with the sailor's cap looked at us with open curiosity as we humped our baggage indoors. The old woman, after one shy look, disappeared indoors.

'I bet,' said I, as we were finishing our tea, 'there's a ghost in this house.'

'Rubbish,' said my mother. 'I've lived forty years, in prehistoric houses and in new bungalows, and I've never had one supernatural experience.'

'An old sailor with a wooden leg,' I said. 'He must have been a pirate. He has a patch on one eye. Under that flagstone is buried his chest of gold!'

'None of this talk!' cried Matilda. 'I won't sleep tonight.'

'There's a ghost all right,' said Maud. 'A tall dark lady. She died of love. She appears out there when the moon's full.' (And Maud pointed to the little yard of the house, built over the sea.)

Matilda covered her ears and ran out of the house, leaving the remnants of her egg and chips on the plate.

'I said, that's enough!' said my mother, quite sharply. 'I want no fighting on this holiday.'

After a brief silence my eldest sister Maria, who all that year had been immersed in the poems of Shelley, said, 'No *individual* ghosts—of course not. There is the One Spirit of the Universe, out of which we came and to which we shall return.'

My mother poured us all another cup of tea.

After the third day, I said to myself, 'This is the very lousiest holiday I've ever had! It is, it is!' And I threw another lonely stone into the lonely sea.

My mother was away all day, from 9 a.m. till near sunset, digging up old Viking stones as if they were jewels.

My sisters went their own ways. Maria did water-colours; pale insipid things with too much of the 'spirit of the universe' in them for my taste. Matilda and Maud were forever with ponies and pony lovers at a farm across the bay.

For three days there was no one on that pier but myself and the old neighbour man who glared at me from his wicker chair beside his door.

(It was high summer—all the boys of Hamnavoe, it seemed, had gone south to the cities on holiday—or to youth camps, or conferences, or a music school.)

I got tired of speaking to gulls and the old man's black

cat (though it was a nice creature that rubbed its head on my knuckles, and sang to me).

I summoned courage one morning to speak to the wicked-looking old man. I approached him diagonally and deviously, with many lingerings and turnings, and brief examinations of clouds and buttercups.

At last the confrontation could not be delayed. He puffed at his pipe and spat. He smelt of rum.

'Tell me,' I stammered, 'about the ghost on this pier, the old pirate.'

He glared at me. One eye was grey and one was green. His face was bristly as a thistle for want of a shave.

'Ghost!' he yelled. 'What ghost? What nonsense is this! What does a whipper-snapper like you know about ghosts!' (He gave a snort and a puff at his pipe and a spit.) 'There's plenty of trouble in the world without ghosts, believe you me. There's old women, for example—always nagging and grousing. . . . That barman, he refused me a last glass of rum because I was a shilling short . . . me, his best customer! That barman's worse than any ghost. Ghosts are good compared to living folk, if you ask me!'

He took three mighty puffs of his pipe, and spat such a gob it half drowned a daisy growing between the flagstones of the pier in tobacco poison.

At this point I was aware that a third party had joined the dialogue (if you could call it that).

It was old Betsy, the misanthrope's wife. She was holding a white plate with a slice of gingerbread on it. 'Here,' she said, smiling. 'It's good.'

She was a good old lady, Betsy.

Old Fred glared malevolently into silence; his pipe crackled and reeked; he stank of stale rum.

At last, on the fifth day, I found a friend!

I was sitting at the edge of the pier, my feet dangling

over the water, trying to catch those small silver-grey fish
they call 'sillocks'.

I caught nothing. There were plenty of sillocks in the
water—shoals of them—legions. But they ignored my
baited hook.

I turned. There was a boy sitting a metre away from
me, his brown legs dangling, looking deep into the water
that flung up into his face a web of shifting gleams.

'O hullo,' I said, surprised.

He smiled, but said nothing.

As if this strange boy's appearance had put a kind of
spell on the sillocks, one after another they bit on bait and
barb and I swung them on to the pier, little glittering
flashes. I had never been so excited! These were the first
fish I had ever caught.

Soon I had a score of sillocks beside me on the edge of
the pier—some tarnished in death, a few feebly slither-
ing, the newest-caught ones twisting and gleaming still
in the sun.

There, all of a sudden, was the black cat Tinker. Tinker
was like a miser with bars of silver, over that scattering of
sillocks. How Tinker sang!

But the boy with the corn-coloured hair, he was no
longer there. He had vanished as silently as he had come.

I took the sillocks to show to old Fred who was of
course sitting outside in his chair.

'Pretty good, boy,' he said. 'You're learning. We'll
make a fisherman of you yet.'

Old Betsy was suddenly in the door, this time with a
glass of ginger ale in her hand.

'Pier sillocks,' said the old man. 'No good. Poor things.
You want to try dropping a line out there, at the mouth
of the harbour. There you haul the big ones you can
fry for your supper. Those things—pooh!—only fit
for cats.'

Betsy said, 'You can use our rowing boat, on the slip

down there, any time you want. But don't go too far out. It's dangerous—the tide-race. . . .'

'It's funny,' I said, handing the empty glass back,' the fish only started to bite after that boy came and sat beside me.'

'Boy?' said old Fred. 'What boy? I've been here all morning and I saw no boy. I don't like boys. Boys aren't welcome here.'

The weather continued fine. At last I got tired of fishing for sillocks.

I availed myself of the offer to use the old man's rowing boat, *Sheena*. After a few splashes and zigzags along the harbour front, I found I could handle the oars quite well.

There are two uninhabited little green islands across the water from the town. The idea occurred to me that I would, after breakfast next morning, take a parcel of egg and cheese and tomato sandwiches, and a few bottles of lemonade, and row to the outer island and have there a little private picnic to myself.

My mother had gone with a trowel to her ancient stones twenty kilometres away. My sisters were busy with horses, or trying to interpret 'the spirit of the universe' by means of water-colours.

Old Fred sat in his chair, puffing furiously—a sign that he was in a bad mood this morning.

Tinker the cat eyed me from the garden wall with golden eyes.

I had hardly got the *Sheena* into the water, when I was aware of the strange boy sitting in the stern. I fixed the oars into the rowlocks and turned the *Sheena* round.

'Hello,' I said, 'how on earth did you get on board?'

Again, no words: only that enchanting smile, as if all the freshness and transient beauty of a summer were gathered into one young face.

I cannot say how glad I was that he was there, sharing the boat with me.

On that green islet we passed the happiest day of my life. We bathed in the sea, on the far side of the islet. We ran about in the sun and wind till we were dry. Those sandwiches—no venison, no royal swan, no sturgeon have ever (I believe) tasted so marvellous, with silver soundless sea music all around! Nor was any champagne or vintage claret like our three shared bottles of lemonade.

Meantime, the ferry boat from the south isles entered the harbour, and a blue fishing boat and a white fishing boat came from the Atlantic with screaming tumults of gulls at the stern of each.

We rowed back through the bow waves of the larger ferry from Scotland, the *St Ola*. The *Sheena* dipped and soared so alarmingly that for a second or two I feared we would be swamped. I knew my face was blanched! My friend laughed delightedly. Soon we were in quiet water again, making oar-swirls and oar-plangencies on the mirror gleams of the bay.

As soon as the *Sheena* touched the slipway, the boy was up and off. . . .

Old Fred had dropped off to sleep in his chair. His cold pipe was in his hand.

I knocked at the door. I told Betsy what a wonderful day it had been. I thanked her for the loan of the boat. 'But I wouldn't have had such a fine time,' I said, 'if it hadn't been for that boy.'

'What boy?' said the kind old lady. 'Weren't you alone?'

It struck me that he had never told me his name. He had never in fact uttered a single word. (The strangeness of it came on me suddenly.)

'I don't know,' I said. 'He has kind of corn-coloured hair.'

Old Betsy looked at me wonderingly.

The old man snored and snored like a blunt saw going through wood.

'There are no boys like that hereabouts,' said Betsy. 'Not that I know about.' (There was, I thought, a slight tremor about her gentle withered mouth.)

'He's dumb,' I said. 'I'm sure he's dumb.'

She went on shaking her head.

'I think,' said Betsy a week or so later, 'I've never seen such a good summer as this, no, not even when I was a small girl. You're lucky. Some summers can be cold bleak times, believe me.'

My mother and my three sisters, coming home each evening from their various avocations, looked increasingly like gypsies. The sun had soaked deeply, too, into the backs of my hands and into my long lean legs. Drying my face each morning, a kind of wild Indian face flashed back at me from the mirror.

There was no more talk of ghosts in our house. The freedom of the four living elements was enough for us.

Only the old man in his basket chair seemed to be unhappy. 'Rheumatics!' he snarled. 'Rheumatics is in my shoulder this year—first time I've had rheumatics there. Like a piece of rusty barbed wire going back and fore, back and fore, through the bones.'

I murmured that I hoped he'd soon be better.

'Believe me, boy,' said he, 'never wish to be an old man like me. It's not desirable—it's by no manner of means to be wished for. If it wasn't for my rum and my pipe, I couldn't carry on another week.'

'You're not half thankful enough,' said Betsy. She appeared briefly at the door, threw a handful of crumbs to the birds, then turned to go indoors again. 'You're a selfish ungrateful old man, and you always have been.'

Fred snarled and cut some black twist tobacco into his palm with a blunt shiny knife blade.

'There's only one thing worse than age,' he said, 'and that's to be cut off in your youth—yes, to be taken suddenly, the way some ignorant yokel tears a rose from a bush in passing.'

I could have sworn there were two tear-drops then, one in each wicked old eye. But it might only have been those worn prisms quivering in the sun.

I even got bored with the *Sheena*, after a week or ten days of puttering about in the harbour alone. My silent friend, the handsome golden-haired one, had not come back since the picnic on the island.

Why should I feel forsaken, almost bereaved, because a boy whose name I did not know was as rare and unpredictable as a shower of rain or a sunburst on water?

Those days when he wasn't there were at last bleak and empty, however the great red jar of the sun tilted its splendours of light and warmth over the summer islands.

A week passed; ten days. Still he didn't come. I might have taken the opportunity to explore the little town and the shores and hills round about; but I felt that if I were away from the pier, even for an hour, he might have come and gone again.

So, day after golden day, I lingered about the pier and endured the grumblings of the old man.

Sometimes he came back from the inn reeking of rum, and then he was more awkward and bad-tempered than ever. And it didn't make a whit of difference to him whether Betsy chided him or spoke kindly to him.

Always she had (smiling) a handful of sweets for me, or a glass of her homemade lemonade.

'It's lonely for you here,' she said. 'Nobody to speak to

but Tinker and the gulls and that old drunken thing. You should take the bus to Kirkwall some morning and see St Magnus Cathedral. Or the ferryboat that goes through Scapa Flow to the south isles. It isn't good for boys to be lonely.'

I couldn't tell this nice old lady what kept me at the stone pier, day after day.

At nights I dreamed often about my friend whose name I had never got to know. They were such strange beautiful dreams as I have never had before or since. Always, in those dreams, the gold-headed boy brimmed over with happiness—I had never known such joy and excitement in my own life. And in every dream he was urging me to join him. 'Come!' he'd cry. 'Come now, quickly!' And I longed to go with him, along the shores and the bird-haunted lochs and hills; but in the dreams I could not go, I seemed to be enchanted like the knight-at-arms to this one small area of wave-washed stones, the pier, and the slipway, and the yard, and our empty house.

In one dream he was carrying a zinc bucket, and it was half full of shellfish that he'd gathered from the rock pools: winkles, mussels, limpets. 'Look!' he cried. 'Look at this lot—if you were with me we'd have twice as many.' (I longed to be with him—I could not move—it was as if I stood drenched in honey.)

Once he was on a hillside, in the dream—he had been gathering flowers: lupins, meadowsweet, marigolds, ox-eye daisies, iris. His face was mysterious and veiled with the fragrant shadows. 'There's more here than I can carry!' he shouted into the wind. 'I've got the whole of summer in my arms—look, too much; there's a marigold fallen! You must come and help me. Please. . . .'

I was shackled as always, to my grey ordinary world.

Was it dew on his face, or tears?

The strange thing is that, though the boy had never

uttered a word to me in our few daytime encounters, in the dreams his voice rang like a new, sweet, wind-hung bell, vibrant with the joy of being alive in that high bounteous summer between boyhood and youth: the one golden time, I have learned since, that knows no shame or guilt. 'Come,' he cried. 'Do you want to grow old and ugly like old Skipper Fred?'

In the last dream, I was walking on a desolate beach. I was miserable. I was in search of my mother and sisters. I wanted them home with me, for a strange reason: I felt threatened without them. (This was unusual—generally, I was glad when they kissed me goodbye and went to their horses, old stones, water colours, once the breakfast dishes had been stacked away.) In the dream—as I walked on the wet sand—I longed bitterly for them.

The boy was suddenly there, in the dream. He was carrying in his arms a great white silent sea bird. 'In a few days,' he said, and his words were heartbreakingly beautiful among the sea sounds, the Atlantic crashings and whisperings and lullings—'Next week, some morning, you and I are going to the crags. Look at that cliff there, to the north—the Black Crag—that's where we'll go, you and I, just the two of us. There's nothing finer in the world, boy, than to hang there between the clouds and the waves. You go from niche to niche, up and down, and across, and the birds are a white shrieking choir all about your head! Promise you'll come.'

'I'll try,' I said, 'but I find it hard to get away.'

He laughed. 'You'll come,' he said. 'We'll be free as the birds for ever.'

Then the white bird in his arms began to thrash and struggle. It shrieked in the boy's face! It half broke from him. One of its wings covered his mouth. . . . In that moment of lyrical brutishness, I woke up to a desolation of spirit I had never known before. . . .

Three more days passed. I hung about the pier more
discontented than ever. Still the sun was a great loom of
brightness in the south. Three barren dreamless nights
passed. I rose to breakfast with four chattering coffee-
swilling letter-reading women.

The old man Fred was grumpier than ever. Even old
Betsy seemed subdued as the first days of August came
in.

I decided, suddenly, that I'd had enough of hanging
blankly about this pier. I would take Betsy's advice and
do a bit of exploring.

I left the pier after breakfast. The women of the house
had already gone. Tinker the cat chased a butterfly under
the washing line.

I took the road round the shore of Hoy Sound. There
are two islands lying to the south across a ramping
turbulent tide-race—Graemsay, a small green island
with a scatter of crafts and two lighthouses, and Hoy
with its soaring blue-scarred glacier-rounded hills. Betsy
had told me about the beach called Warbeth that was nice
for picnics and bathing and rock-pool rifling, and about
the Black Crag, a dangerous place, that lay beyond.
'Keep well back from the Black Crag!' she had warned
me, shaking a finger.

On I walked, among the sea gleams and the lulling sea
sounds.

What Betsy hadn't told me was that the road led past
the local cemetery, or kirkyard, or (as the oldest people
had called it in their quaint way) 'God's acre'.

This black honeycomb of death made me pause. The
yard of a thousand stones: I couldn't bring myself to skirt
the outer wall of it, even, though the Atlantic lay on the
far side, open and free. The marvellous ocean music was
already in my ears.

I was in the act of turning back when I saw the boy in
the kirkyard, all alone. He seemed to be lingering round

one stone in particular. I called out to him. He paid no attention. There was a most astonishing expression on his face: wonderment, fear, a kind of dawning joy. Once he reached out with his finger and touched the stone.

I called out to him again. He paid no attention. I ran—I stumbled in my hurry—I bruised my knee on a kerb—to get through the gate and be with him. 'Wait, I'm coming! Here—it's me! I'll go wherever you want. . . .'

He was not there. There was no one there, in the kirkyard on this beautiful summer morning, but myself.

I searched everywhere for him. He had fled like a shadow—it seemed he might have merged into the stone.

I returned at last to the tomb he had been lingering at. Under a list of ancient worn Victorian names, this was cut:

IVOR SINCLAIR
Died aged 11 years
as the result of an accident
5th August 1911

Butterflies tumbled silently among the graves. From the rocks below came the Atlantic whisper, again and again. The ripening cornfield on the slope above sent its multitudinous whisperings among the stones of the God-acre.

It was early afternoon when I got back to our pier. There was no sign of old Fred. I didn't have to wait long for an explanation. 'Drunk!' said Betsy. 'He went to the inn at opening time and he spent all his pension money before dinner—every last penny! Two fishermen carted the old villain home. *I don't want him,* I said to them. *Throw him on the bed there. He'll come to in his own time. Silly old fool!—I hope he has a splitting headache. . . .'*

I had never seen Betsy so upset. But, upset or not, she hastened indoors to fetch me shortbread and ginger ale.

'He always gets drunk on the fifth of August,' she said. 'That's to say, he gets ten times drunker on the fifth of August than he is most days. Something happened—oh, a long time ago—when he was just about the age you are now. I don't suppose you want to hear about it—why should you? Well, I'll tell you all the same. Fred had a twin brother, and by all accounts they were very close. They went everywhere together. They were inseparable. They fished together and they flew kites together. At Hallowe'en they lit fires and they did all sorts of mischief. . . . Well, then, it was the summer holidays. One morning they decided to go to the crags. In those days, seventy years ago, it was nothing for men and boys to go to the cliffs. All that great crag knowledge is lost now. Fred and this brother of his, they had done it hundreds of times before. Nobody worried about them. . . . Well, this very day seventy years ago—fifth of August in the year 1911—Fred came back from the Black Crag alone. Late in the evening he came back, to this very house on this very pier, grey as a ghost, and not able to speak. At last he managed to say that a great white bird had flown at his brother and knocked him off a ledge.

'They found Ivor's body next day at the foot of the crag, all broken.'

A week later, my mother and sisters and I left Orkney.

The sea gateway out of Orkney is guarded by two immense crags, one on each side, the Kame of Hoy and Black Crag.

I sat on the deck of the *St Ola* with Maria. Of my three sisters she was the one I had got to know best over the last few days. We were muffled in thick coats and bonnets and scarves; for at last the golden idyll had broken, and wind whined in the rigging and spindrift was blown from the crests of the waves.

I told Maria the story of the boy Ivor who had suffered a cliff death so long ago: without, of course, mentioning my own dealings with that ghost and dream creature. 'Life is cruel,' I declared. 'It isn't fair. I'll never understand it. . . .'

Maria quoted some poetry (Shelley, of course):

> He is made one with Nature; there is heard
> His voice in all her music, from the moan
> Of thunder, to the song of night's sweet bird.
> He is a presence to be felt and known
> In darkness and in light, in herb and stone,
> Moving itself where'er that Spirit doth move
> Which hath withdrawn his being to its own,
> Which wields the world with never-wearied love,
> Sustains it from beneath, and kindles it above.

The boat moved to the open colder waters. A thong of spindrift lashed my face; it left a marvellous taste of salt.

The Devil's Laughter

JAN NEEDLE

There was a typhoid scare on when the Boyd family flew out for their Greek island holiday, and everyone in England was being nervous, and getting jabs, and being silly as usual. The Boyds, who had travelled a lot, and to some pretty hairy places, laughed. All those Greeks, plus a few million tourists, and a mere three people had contracted the disease—what was the panic? You had more chance of getting trampled by an elephant at the zoo.

Danny Boyd's grandmother, however, was perturbed. 'He's only seven,' she protested. 'And he's such a beautiful little boy. You'd never forgive yourselves if anything happened to him.'

Danny blushed, because even at that age he did not like to be described as beautiful. It did not help that his two sisters laughed at him, and pointed their fingers.

'Beautiful, Beautiful!' squawked Sarah, who was thirteen and horrible. 'Don't worry, Grandma, no self-respecting typhoid germ would go anywhere near that dirty little boy!'

Grandma, who was quite old, and rather posh, looked 'vexed' as she would call it. 'Too beautiful to live,' she muttered.

But the family chuckled at her, in a friendly way. They were not bothering.

'No harm will come to Danny,' said Dad, ruffling his blonde, curly hair. 'Will it, Dan? It would take more than dirty water to kill this one.'

'He's afraid of ghosts,' said Vicky. She was nicer than Sarah, Danny thought. She was eleven and liked rough games. 'But I suppose you don't get them out there. Too hot.'

This caused a discussion, because to Sarah and Dad it seemed wrong that you couldn't have ghosts in a hot climate. But Mum, Danny, Grandma and Vicky were certain. For ghosts, you needed ruined houses, and howling winds, and cold, dripping cellars. The idea of a sunshine spook was crazy. Nobody howled eerily in the Mediterranean nights. Above a certain temperature, Vicky insisted, ghosts were impossible.

'You're safe then, Danny,' said Sarah. 'Pity really. It would be doing the world a service if you were spirited away!'

'Sarah!' said Gran. 'If you joke about *everything* something bad will happen. It's bound to.'

Danny, for no rational reason at all, felt a stir of fear.

When their plane touched down at the airport on Zakinthos, all these things had been forgotten. They arrived in the afternoon, and their parents' friend Nikos was waiting for them. He festooned their luggage all over his car, chatted to Dad, kissed Mum and hugged the children, and thundered off along the coast road to Akrotiri in a style that made the girls and Danny gasp, but which the adults appeared to accept as normal. The last two kilometres were up rough country lanes of dried mud, through acres and acres of bent and stunted trees which mother said bore olives. Even over the noise of the engine, and Nikos, they were aware of a weird sound—a harsh, high-pitched chirping. When they halted by a small white house and the engine was switched off, it almost overwhelmed them.

'But what *is* it?' said Danny. 'It sounds like a hundred babies saying choo-choo! A thousand babies! All the babies in the world!'

'It is cicadas,' said Nikos. 'Here in the olive trees there are millions of them. You get used to it.'

The whole family listened, amazed, for quite a while. The noise was loud, and insistent, and constant. It did sound something like Danny had said, but only something. It was indescribable.

'Don't they ever stop?' asked Danny.

'At night,' replied Nikos. 'They like the sun on them. From evening until the sun is well up in the morning they are silent. Look, I'll show you one.'

Danny and Vicky and Sarah followed him to a tree.

'Look,' said Nikos. 'Who can find one first?'

They stared and stared, but could see nothing. Yet the noise was so loud that their ears were ringing with it.

'No,' said Vicky. 'Are you certain there are any in this tree?'

Nikos pointed a brown stubby finger at the rough bark. When it was almost touching the tree, Danny squeaked.

'I can see it! It's *horrible!*'

It was like a cross between a huge wasp and a very fat fly, and it was beautifully camouflaged. As they stared, it started up its noise, without apparently moving or opening its mouth. It gazed glassily at them with brown bright eyes, as if indifferent.

The noise was irregular for a moment or two, until the creature had picked up the rhythm of the other cicadas in the tree. Which was the rhythm of them all. The noise surged upwards to a crescendo. Thousands, millions, of cicadas making the same harsh, rhythmic double note.

'It's like laughter,' said Danny. He looked sickened, fearful. 'It's like some horrible, nasty laughter.'

Sarah put on a face.

'Devil's laughter,' she said. She made a claw of her hand and snatched at Danny's eyes. 'It's long-dead souls. They'll climb into your hair at nightime and suck your brains out through your ears.'

Danny, to the embarrassment of Nikos, burst into tears and rushed into the house.

'They're completely harmless,' he told the girls, as if apologizing. 'They just sit in the trees all day and make this noise, I don't know why. They do not seem to have a purpose.'

Before he left the family to it, the Greek shared a glass of wine and a chat with the grown-ups. Mum and Dad had been to Zakinthos before, on business and pleasure, and they knew several of the locals. The children listened to some of the talk, but not seriously. It all sounded pretty routine.

'Oh,' said Nikos, as he walked into the sunshine. 'Dino. Things are bad with him.'

'Dino?' said mother.

'You know,' said Dad. 'The shepherd. What's up with him?'

'His son,' replied Nikos. 'Cristos. He is dead. He died three months ago.'

'Oh *no*,' said Mum. 'But he was only . . .'

'Seven years old,' said Nikos, gravely. 'The same age as your Daniel I remember. The same month even, I think.'

'Yes,' said father. 'February. What did the little chap die of?'

'He . . . I do not know,' said Nikos. 'He seemed to . . . to waste away somehow. He faded. Like a . . . like a flower. Then he died.'

The children were studying the faces of their parents. In the fly-buzzing warmth of the small white-washed kitchen, the atmosphere was oddly cold. There was nothing said for many seconds. The grinding rasp of the cicadas filled the air.

'Poor Cristos,' said Mother. 'Poor Dino.'

'He has taken it cruelly,' said Nikos. 'I must warn you. He is changed. Be careful.'

Again the sense of chill.

'Careful?' said Mum. 'How do you mean exactly?'

'I do not know, exactly,' said Nikos. 'I am sorry. I am spoiling your day. But . . . be careful.'

'But Dino is such a . . .' began Mother.

'Lovely, fantastic, man,' said Dad.

'To lose a son, in this country,' said Nikos. He gave a half smile to the girls. 'A daughter, for a man like Dino, would have been not . . . not quite so . . .'

'Poor Dino,' said mother. 'Thank you, Nikos. Thank you for telling us.'

By the time the shepherd turned up one morning, four days later, Danny, Sarah and Vicky had come to adore the little house, and the countryside, and the places they had seen.

The house was not like anything they knew at home. It was single storey, and very small, with two tiny bedrooms and a tinier place yet where Danny slept. It had neither water nor electricity, nor any form of plumbing. At first the children were thrown by this, quite put out. But their parents laughed at them, and told them they were talking like tourists. If they wanted to see another country properly, and experience how completely *different* it was, what was the point of staying in a hotel that could have been in Margate? The children, catching the logic, took the toilet roll and the spade into the olive grove when they needed to—and ended up enjoying it.

They soon became expert cicada spotters, and if the noise got too insistent in the heat of the afternoon, they would patrol the trees nearest the house and touch the lethargic fat creatures with the tip of a stick until they'd buzzed off—literally—to a more distant perch. This way they could cut the noise level considerably, and the 'devil's laughter' would be less fearsome, if just as eerie. They hunted up scorpions at the well, and had competitions every day to see who could surprise the biggest lizard basking on a rock.

Best of all they liked the beaches. Their parents hired a Citroen Pony, a type of mini-jeep with an open top and clattering engine, and they zoomed all over the place. By British standards the beaches they visited were empty, and each one had a taverna where they had beer and kebabs and ice-cream and gallons of lemonade. The water was clear and warm, and the sunshine lasted till well after Danny's bedtime. Despite the heat and the mosquitos—kept at bay with odd green spirals which smoked and smouldered redly beside their beds all night, the children slept like logs.

It was a Sunday morning that they met Dino, and he came past the house while they were still in bed. They heard him first, by the flat clanking of sheep bells, and a peculiar, mournful noise of music. Romantic Vicky thought it must be pan pipes, which she'd read about in *The Wind in the Willows*. When it got nearer, though, the noise revealed itself as a very cheap old tranny, playing the sort of stuff appropriate to a Sunday. Sarah laughed, of course.

Danny was still mouldering in his pit, so the parents and the girls went outside to greet the shepherd. At first they saw only sheep, big, skinny, rangy animals quite unlike anything they'd come across in England, more like goats in fact, which nibbled energetically at the dried-up grass they found at the bases of the trees. When Dino detached himself from the gnarled old olive trunk he had been leaning against Sarah and Vicky jumped. He'd been like part of it.

The shepherd came slowly forward, his face expressionless. He was a tall, gaunt man, with brown-burnt skin and drifts of hair wisping out from underneath an odd leather hat. He wore blue trousers, sandals, and a stained brown open shirt. His massive chest was covered in curly white hair. As he approached, an aura of quiet, wistful music emanated from somewhere about him, some pocket where the tiny radio was hidden.

'Dino,' said father quietly, then spoke in Greek for a while. The shepherd did not smile, although his eyes gazed directly at them. His eyes were very brown; and, to the girls, almost unbearably sad.

Mother spoke to the shepherd then, and Dad once more. Vicky and Sarah glanced at each other. Was this going to get embarrassing? Why did this huge, sad man not answer? Was he going to merely stare at them until they smarted, then go on his way? Father and mother stopped talking. Dad shifted his weight uneasily from one leg to the other. The cicadas found a crescendo. The harsh double note began to batter at their ears, each one of the millions perfectly in time. It was uncomfortably mocking, peculiarly deliberate.

Then Danny appeared in the doorway, pushing sleepily between his sisters onto the step, blinking blindly in the powerful sunshine. Danny, small and beautiful, with a mass of golden curls, with one sandal on and a pair of dirty white shorts, nothing else. The cicadas, as if by magic, stopped. The noise faded almost to nothing. In the quiet chirrupping that was left, the shepherd spoke.

'Boy,' he said. His voice was choked, emotional. They all looked at him, startled, except Danny, who was half asleep, still blinking. 'Oh, boy. Boy. Boy.'

His face was terrifying, racked with pain. His mouth was half open, and his eyes were liquid and beseeching. In the trees behind him the cicadas found a new rhythm. The noise built up to a new, violent, beating laughter.

'Dino,' said mother uncertainly. 'This is our son. Our

Daniel.' She pushed him further forward, onto the step, into the sun.

'Danny. Say hello. It's Dino. He's the shepherd.'

Dino left them then, with hardly another word being spoken. But he returned that evening, with a large bottle of his own rough white wine, and a bundle of cheese and olives. They all sat out on the step and Dino talked to them. He was a changed man.

His English was not perfect, but he spoke it with a fluid humour that was completely charming. He knew how to turn a phrase to make the English laugh, and he could speak rapidly and fluently when he needed to, bringing the funny parts of his stories into comic relief. He also had a superb knack of knowing what the children liked to hear. If Sarah and Vicky were enthralled, Danny was bewitched.

The shepherd told comic tales of the characters he had known on the island, and bizarre tales of the war—like the hurling of sixty men and women off the cliff at Kampi because they had collaborated with the Germans. He told them stories of fishing in great storms, of visitations of dread diseases, of the eccentric behaviour of the tourists since the jet planes started flying them in. He was relaxed, and friendly, and laughing, his eyes no longer sad, no longer haunting. When he stood up to go it was pitch dark, and the cicadas had long been silent. Now the sounds were the sighing of the wind in the olive groves, and the occasional crackle as the fire they had built died down. Dino shook hands with mother and father, and bowed gravely at the girls.

Then he touched Danny lightly on the cheek.

'Perhaps you would like to come with me tomorrow? To help me tend the sheep?'

Mother gave a light laugh.

'Oh I don't think so, Dino,' she said. 'We're off to the

beach near Volimes tomorrow. It would take wild horses to keep him away from there.'

Danny surprised them all.

'I don't want to go swimming, Mum,' he said. 'I want to go with Dino.'

Dino bent and kissed him lightly among the curls on the top of his head.

'Good,' he said. 'I will call you at six o'clock.'

'Six!' said Sarah. 'But little sleepyhead won't . . .'

'I'll be up,' said Danny. 'Leave me alone, Sarah.'

When Dino left, the girls tried to rib him about it, but it didn't work. Somehow they felt uncomfortable. Everybody did.

Except Danny.

And when they arose next morning, he was gone. The dawn was still red in the sky.

That evening, Dino brought Danny home at eight o'clock. He was carrying him, and Danny was asleep. The big shepherd laid him onto the pile of rugs that was his bed, while the family looked on like strangers. Mother, unable to stop herself, shook Danny's head gently, and woke him.

'Did you have a nice time, darling?' she asked, strangely anxious.

Danny's eyes were dazed, but his smile was radiant.

'Yes,' he said. 'I want to go again tomorrow.'

He fell asleep again immediately, and Dino sat down at the rough wood table to chat. Mother seemed absurdly curious to know what they had done all day. The Greek smiled slowly.

'We followed the sheep,' he said. 'We talked. It was like old times.'

Long into the night, Sarah and Vicky heard their parents talking in the room next door. Quietly but anxiously. The girls could not understand what they were worried about.

'If the daft little twit wants to sit on a rock all day and listen to stories, that's his lookout,' said Sarah. 'At least it keeps him out of *our* hair, doesn't it?'

'I wonder what he meant,' mused Vicky. 'It was like old times?'

'Oh shut up, Vick,' said Sarah. 'You're as bad as mum and dad you are. There's no mystery. They just like each other, that's all. Old Dino likes our baby brother. I can't *imagine* why!'

'His son was seven,' said Vicky. 'I wonder if that's what he meant. The one that died.'

'You could always ask him, Nosy,' replied her sister. 'Now shut up, will you? I'm asleep.'

Next day, although he woke up early, Danny was surprised to find his mother already in the kitchen. She told him that he was not going out with Dino that day, that she and his father had discussed it and decided on a family outing to the beach. Danny grinned and shrugged.

'All right,' he said. 'Great.'

Mum felt a complete idiot. She'd expected tears, or fury, or a fight. Why? She blushed.

'You can go with Dino some other day, of course,' she said. 'How will that do?'

'Yeah,' said Danny. 'Let's dig the girls out shall we? We can get to Tsilivi earlier than *anybody* else! You wake Dad up!'

The change was subtle, but complete. Within six days the girls were rattled, father was looking strained, and mum was getting desperate. Something was wrong, something terrible was happening. But what? And why? And how? There was nothing to catch hold of, nothing visible. But something awful was taking place. Something dreadful was being done.

It was noticeable, although not obvious, by the end of the day at Tsilivi. Danny, during the morning, had been his usual delirious self at the seaside. He'd played ball with the Greek children, he'd swum through the surf for hours on the Lilo, he'd explored the rocky pools at the headlands, he'd eaten ice-cream and drunk coke. But during the afternoon, he became listless, bored. Dad, swimming along the shore, had come across him on the Lilo, just floating, not moving a muscle, lying on his back with his eyes open, staring at the sky. And he had spoken to him—from the side of the air bed—three times before Danny had replied.

That evening, Dino turned up, and chatted and enchanted them as before. He brought wine and fresh local cheese, and a small gift for the girls and Danny—lovely little wooden figures that he had carved himself. At the end of the evening he asked if Danny could go with him next day, to tend the sheep, and Danny bubbled over with excitement.

What could his parents say? Dino was warm, and smiling, and friendly and they'd had a superb evening because of him. They said yes, of course. But don't keep him out so late this time, Dino, please. It did not suit him.

'No,' said Dino. 'Home by six o'clock. For the English tea!'

Everybody laughed. But in bed, even Sarah was uneasy. When Vicky raised the subject, she almost bit her head off. . . .

On his return the next evening, Danny was too sleepy, much too sleepy, for 'the English tea'. Dino, as before, put him to bed. This time he kissed him on the cheek and spoke to him, quietly, in Greek. Danny smiled, and answered. He was also speaking Greek. But when Sarah squeaked, and remarked on this phenomenon, Dino did not smile. He looked at her quite coldly. He stayed only for a few minutes more, then left. He did not ask if Danny could accompany him tomorrow.

Three days later the first really frightening thing occurred. Danny almost drowned. And if it had not been so ridiculous, the family might have admitted to themselves that it seemed in a horrible way inevitable. Even . . . deliberate.

It happened at the rocky beach near Volimes. They had gone there because up to now it had been their favourite. Especially Danny's. They had snorkels and flippers, and the beach was so isolated that they always swum in the nude, the lot of them. There was a tiny cafe there, a tumbledown house among the rocks, owned by an old old lady who served only eggs fried in deep olive oil and warm beer in dirty glasses. The road down was ridiculous, a dusty rutted track so steep that mother had to sit on the bonnet of the Pony going back up to give the front-wheel drive some weight to grip with. Nobody else went there at all. They'd never seen a soul.

They went there this time because it was Danny's favourite place, where he'd once even seen a small octopus lurking in the rocks. They hoped desperately it might interest him, might take his mind off the night before. Might make him behave like part of them again, like the happy, normal little boy they knew and—even Sarah would admit it now—loved.

They had had a row the evening before, in which Danny had behaved in a way that had shocked and frightened them. It had started, inevitably, with Dino. He had spent the evening with the family, and it had been disastrous. Mother, by now, could hardly talk to him without trembling, and father seemed on the point of anger all the time. The girls, polite and lost, still listened to his stories, but they were most uncomfortable, almost afraid. Dino was not talking to them any more. Or to their parents. He was talking to Danny. The two of them were in a world enclosed, they were alone in the company, they were a pair who deliberately shut the others out.

When Dino had gone, and Danny was lying in his bed, he announced that he was going to the hills again tomorrow.

'Who says?' snapped father. 'I don't recall hearing that arranged.'

'I arranged it,' said Danny. 'With Dino. With my *patera*.'

Although the girls did not understand it, this seemed to be a key word. Father's tanned face became abruptly pale, and mother let out a squawk. Within seconds there was bellowing, Danny was out of bed and scratching and biting at his parents, and Vicky was in tears. It was horrible and unsettling, and the upshot was that Danny was made to sleep in with his parents because he refused to say that he would not slip out of the house before dawn. Before they passed into unhappy and exhausted sleep, Sarah got Vicky to look up the word in her Greek dictionary. It meant father.

Danny almost drowned after he paddled the Lilo off among the rocks all by himself. He was pale and sick-looking this morning, but he—like the rest of the family—chose to ignore last night, chose to pretend that nothing had happened. When asked where he was going on the Lilo, he said, 'To look for that octopus again'. His father, smiling a strained smile, said, 'Fine. Make sure he doesn't have you for his breakfast!'

And fifteen minutes later, quite by accident, totally by luck, Sarah and Vicky happened to be standing on a high rock, and they saw their brother underwater—drowning.

He did not have his face mask on, nor his flippers. He

was about two metres under, and he was on his back, with his eyes open; and his mouth. A small, naked boy with blonde hair streaming in the blue water, drifting slowly downwards into the deep, dark shadows among the jagged rocks. Through the distortion of the water he appeared to be looking at his sisters on the rock. He appeared to be smiling.

There was more than fear in the screams of Vicky and Sarah. There was a certain kind of horror. When they got back to the house, the cicadas were almost silent. Then, suddenly, they produced a raucous, blastingly loud burst of rhythmic noise. The laughter. It was terribly like laughter. Vicky cried uncontrollably for ten minutes before Dad could calm her down.

It was mother, a brilliant swimmer, who rescued Danny and gave him mouth-to-mouth, and it was mother, a rock once her mind was made up, who got them off the island the very next day, who cut short the holiday, and cut their losses, and booked them a flight to anywhere and damn the expense. She did not tell her husband until she had done it, and she did not tell the children at all. When they returned from the rocky beach, and Danny had been put to bed, she took the Pony and drove to the town. The girls half guessed what she had done, though, and they were glad. They were almost overwhelmed.

Danny was asleep all day, and watched all night. But he did get out, at about three in the morning, when Dad must have nodded off for a time. This time there was no pretending. The girls were woken up and made to search. The four of them, with torches, made towards the knoll above the olive groves where Danny often sat with Dino. They searched with silent determination, and moved fast and fiercely through the sparse, dry, grass. Vicky found her brother, not hiding, but sitting beside a rock, looking at the stars. He was crying, very quietly, and he allowed himself to be led by the hand back to his bed. He would not let his father carry him, or anybody else.

But he had to be carried onto the plane next day. He collapsed at lunchtime when the plan to fly out from Zakinthos was revealed to him. He turned so white, and breathed so shallowly, that he looked dead. The officials at the airport were anxious, thinking he might have some illness. There was still the typhoid scare, they pointed out. The typhoid scare? The family were bemused. It all seemed light years away. They smiled unhappily, and explained. No, not an illness. Their little boy was . . . well, he was not ill, at least.

As they stared through the small square window of the plane, Sarah and Vicky thought they spotted Dino. There was a tall, gaunt figure at the wire fence, in blue and brown. But it was too far to tell, really; much too far. He had a small child with him, a little boy, in shorts and tee shirt, with shining hair. So it could not be Dino, could it? As the jet accelerated, a haze of heat from the engines blotted out the figures.

About two months later, the family received a letter from Zakinthos, from Nikos. It was a long letter, full of news, and regret at their so-sudden parting, which they had half explained in a note. It ended with a peculiar piece of news. Dino the shepherd was dead. He had drowned himself in a lonely, rocky bay near Volimes.

Mother, who was reading the letter aloud, stopped. She looked at her husband, and at Sarah and Vicky. There was silence for some while. Then mother continued to read.

'. . . the most odd is, the old woman who saw him jump into the sea, said there was a child with him, a little boy. She said she even saw him in the water, drifting down and drowning. She insists.'

Mother's voice had almost died away. It was hardly audible.

'But she was wrong, of course. Dino, as you know, had lost his son. And there was no other body found, except for Dino's. It was odd, though, wasn't it? Drifting down, she said, with his hair trailing out like grass. And smiling. She insisted . . .'

After a crushing silence, mother said, 'Ought we to tell Danny, do you think? When we visit on Thursday?'

Sarah and Vicky said nothing. Father sighed.

'I don't know,' he said. 'Will it help, do you think? To know that Dino and . . . to know that Dino's dead? Will it help?'

In the quiet, Vicky spoke loudly. A smile was growing on her face, as if the strain of weeks was being smoothed away. It was a wonderful, shining smile. Her voice was shaky with excitement.

'The cicadas,' she said. 'In my head. They've gone. I can't hear them any more. Oh Mum! Oh Dad! I can't hear them any more!'

Sarah knew what she meant, even if her parents did not. Vicky had not wanted to burden them with her small troubles, this constant laughter in her brain. Sarah smiled.

'Don't worry, Mum,' said Sarah. 'She's not gone mad. Look—let's see Dan tomorrow, can we? Let's not wait till Thursday?'

The girls' elation was infectious. There was a stirring in all four of them. A heady, crazy feeling. Of hope.

'Yes,' said father. 'Why not?'

'Oh Danny,' said Mum. 'My poor lost boy.'

'We're going to find him, Mum,' said Vicky. 'Tomorrow.'

The laughter had gone.

His Coy Mistress

JEAN STUBBS

When I was seventeen and began my Art School training I loved a student in his final year called Hannibal Mundi. That wasn't his real name of course. His father and mother owned a grocer's shop in Salford, their surname was Jackson and they christened him Arnold.

'It was like wearing somebody else's old clothes,' he told me. 'So I chose *Hannibal* because he and his elephants crossed the Alps, and *Mundi* because I belong to the world!'

He ran into constant difficulties with officialdom over his rebaptism, and caused everyone confusion or grief, but all his paintings bore his chosen signature and his friends never thought of him as anyone else.

We met in the art school office. I was buying drawing paper, and he had come in to register for the autumn term a month late.

'The Principal thought you'd turn up sometime, Mr Mundi,' said the secretary, trying not to smile, for Hannibal was wearing a false yellow beard and twirling a striped umbrella, 'and he says he wants a word with you when you do!'

Hannibal placed his umbrella on her desk and his beard on her typewriter, and held out his arms to me as I was trying to find the right change in my purse.

''Tis black-eyed Susan!' he cried. 'Stay, lovely wench, and I will sing to thee.'

Then, falling on one knee, he poured out the first verse of '*Two Lovely Black Eyes*', in the splendid limpid style of an Italian tenor.

'Hush, Mr Mundi!' said the secretary, giggling. 'Oh, do hush!'

I began to laugh, and the more I laughed the more poignantly he sang, and the more the secretary giggled and said, 'Oh, Mr Mundi, do hush!' Until at last the door of the inner sanctum opened, and the Principal came out, taking off his reading glasses. He was a shrewd and pleasant man with a dry sense of humour.

He said, 'I thought that was you, Mundi!'

Hannibal rose to his feet and bowed deeply, but not impudently.

'Far be it from me,' said the Principal ironically, 'to trouble you with such trivial matters as hours or minutes, because I realize that your notion of time is entirely different from mine. In fact I have often wondered whether you use a calendar rather than a clock. But to turn up a whole month late, Mundi, seems excessive, even for you. Is it possible to hope for some improvement in the future?'

'Not in the least, sir,' Hannibal replied, honest but courteous.

'I thought not,' said the Principal. 'So would you kindly shut up and get out and leave me in peace?'

'At once, sir. I crave your pardon, sir. But this blessed damozel, sir, leaned out from the gold bar of heaven.'

The Principal looked at me over his glasses and gave me a piece of sound advice.

'Have nothing to do with this fellow, Miss Davison, unless you nourish an insatiable desire for the unexpected, and a life of chaos.'

My stomach hurt with laughter, and with the holding of laughter. I could not have answered, and what was there to say? I bit my lips and inclined my head, as if to say I thanked him and took his point.

'Come outside with me at once, Susan!' cried Hannibal. 'You have deliberately disturbed the Principal with your singing!'

He swept me out of the office as I started to laugh again.

He was quite the ugliest young man I had ever seen. His friend Bob Brewer, who specialized in cartoons, drew and described him as 'A lamppost with red hair and broken glasses.'

Girls said to him frankly but not unkindly, 'Hey, aren't you revolting?' Then their expressions changed, and you could tell they hoped he thought they were pretty.

But in the corridor that October morning he became serious and delightful, and I felt serious too. He put his hands on either side of my face, and smiled a smile of total recognition.

He said, 'Do you remember an Inn, Miranda?'

He was Mr and Mrs Jackson's only child, and they would have liked him to come into the grocery business with them and take it over when they died, but he disabused them of that notion quite early by showing a remarkable talent for art, and refusing to be good at anything else. I only met them twice, poor souls, but on first acquaintance I couldn't help wondering whether his hospital crib had been switched at birth. In no way did he appear to belong to them.

Mrs Jackson opened the conversation by referring to him as Arnold, and to his gift as though it were a rare disease.

'Arnold got it from his grandad.' she explained. 'Not my side of the family, love—*his* side!' Nodding grimly towards her husband, who was hidden behind his Sunday newspaper. 'Arnold's grandad was a coal miner, but my family was always in respectable trade.'

She jerked her head at one of a shoal of framed

photographs which, over the years, had washed up on the shore of the sideboard.

'That's Grandad Jackson on the right.' Her pause was a criticism. 'Mind you,' she added, 'he was right fond of grandma. One time he painted a bunch of flowers for her because he couldn't afford to buy them. This is him and her, took at Blackpool just before the war.'

The photograph was brown and indistinct, and I could find nothing to say about them, but apparently grandad's painting was still in existence, hanging over Hannibal's bedroom mantlepiece, so I asked if I could see it. Mrs Jackson came up with us to chaperone me.

'You think I'm going to leap on her, don't you?' Hannibal asked.

'You nasty-minded lad!' cried Mrs Jackson, outraged. And to me, 'I hope you'll excuse him, love. It isn't the way *I* brought him up, but he was right fond of grandad, and grandad could be coarse.'

'I loved the old lad,' said Hannibal seriously. 'He slaved away all his life at a job he hated, which killed him in the end. It's a mistake which I have no intention of repeating.'

His mother sighed, and folded her hands in her apron.

'You've got lovely dark hair, love,' she said to me, changing the subject. 'Don't it shine? I *do* like nice clean hair.'

'That remark—though a compliment to you, kiddo—is a reminder to me that I once brought a girl called Shirley home,' said Hannibal. 'Shirley was a sexual mistake of my first year at art school. A generous and understanding wench who didn't wash much.'

'Long and clean like Grandma Jackson's,' his mother continued loudly and firmly over him. 'Ah, she was a lovely woman.'

'What happened to Grandma Jackson?' I asked politely.

I looked resolutely at the painting, because Hannibal was pulling faces to make me laugh, and I was afraid he might succeed. Then the picture absorbed me utterly. It was unique. The man must have loved his wife to paint this fantasy bouquet. They were flowers of no known species, flowers of paradise. Their colours jostled each other in exotic disharmony. A child-like precision of detail suggested that the artist was self-taught, but his gift of expression, like that of his grandson, was rich and strange and wonderful.

'It's not many that can speak well of their mother-in-law,' said Mrs Jackson with mournful pride, 'but I can, and do. She died not a fortnight after him. Yes, married over forty years and had ten children, six of them buried, and never a cross word.'

'Only sheep never have a cross word,' said Hannibal. 'I'll bet they fought like hell and made it up in bed. You don't have all those children without a spot of malarky.'

Mrs Jackson had learned long since that it was better to ignore him. She spoke even louder this time, for the benefit of her husband downstairs in the parlour.

'Yes, Grandad Jackson was a *good* husband. I'll say that for him. He lit the fire for grandma every morning of their married life, and took her a cup of tea in bed.'

The silence from downstairs was noticeable.

'It's no use, mother,' said Hannibal. 'He stopped listening to you years ago.' He turned to me, saying, 'The petty miseries of middle-aged wedlock are not for us. Come into the garden, Maud, for the black bat night has flown!'

My youth and clean hair had raised me in Mrs Jackson's estimation, who was suspicious of her son's friends.

'That's no way to talk to a nice girl! Besides, I thought you said her name was Susan, not Maud.'

'Her name is neither Maud nor Susan, mother. She has

many names. On rare occasions I have even been known to call her Fishface.'

She gave him up as a bad job and spoke to me in a different tone.

'What's your proper name, love?'

'It doesn't matter,' Hannibal said, before I could reply. 'She won't be coming here again. There's no need to exchange credentials.'

To me she said, 'You can come whenever you like, love.' To her son, 'You're not going off courting on a Sunday afternoon looking like that, are you, Arnold? Why don't you comb your hair?'

Hannibal said truthfully, 'What difference would it make?'

No one could ignore him, even passing him by in the street. He roused strong feelings. Some people detested him. Some adored him. Many put up with him. But most judgments were softened by a smile.

'Ah, that fellow's a flight of God's fancy!' said the painting master, who was Hannibal's chief mentor.

I never took him to my home because he would have horrified them. I never met him again at the shop, because he had learned to keep any loved thing to himself. He had no patience with social codes of behaviour, either. If he liked someone he offered his friendship. If he didn't, then he said so. As a couple we were only acceptable in the art-school world, among those who cherished eccentrics.

'What cheek!' cried the pottery master, enjoying a preview of the students' summer exhibition. 'That chap Mundi has put a cat on the wall bang in front of the picture, with its back turned on us. Still, it works. You like breaking rules, don't you, Mundi?'

'What rules?' Hannibal asked, quite sincerely. He added, 'So long as it works, rules don't matter.'

'True,' said the painting master, 'but most of us can't create anything good enough to take their place.'

Hannibal said, 'I can.'

That year he won the Olive Harkness Award for the most promising student, a scholarship to the Royal College of Art, and the painting prize. I wonder what he would have done if he had been able to accept them. We never found out. He died at the end of that summer.

I waited at the bus stop that hot summer day for two long hours, and then I went home and waited for five days because his notion of time was hazy. He had always been unpredictable, and we lived so very far apart in every way. It was also possible that he had changed his mind about me. I tried to understand, and I called on my pride to sustain me, but finally I cycled the familiar distance over to Jackson's Family Grocery, trying to look as though I had just been passing by.

They said he had been buried the day before.

'But he wasn't ill. What did he die of?' I said. 'He was only twenty-two. What *could* he die of?'

'A massive heart attack, the doctor said, love. Massive.' Mrs Jackson was obscurely proud of its size. 'It was as much of a shock to us as it is to you, love.'

'But didn't he speak before he . . . ? Didn't he say anything, leave anything before he . . . ?'

'He died in his sleep, love. Died in his sleep.'

I found myself sitting on a barrel with Mrs Jackson pushing my head down onto my knees, and Mr Jackson fanning me with a sheaf of margarine competition leaflets. They offered me a glass of dark sweet Oporto-type wine. They brought my bicycle inside, because of thieves.

'I'd have let you know, love,' said Mrs Jackson, with genuine kindness, 'but Arnold never even told me your proper name, never mind your address and telephone number. He was always that secretive.'

She said, 'If there's any sort of a souvenir you'd like, to remind you of our Arnold, you're more than welcome to take your pick.'

I couldn't yet take in the fact that he no longer existed, let alone choose something in his memory.

I said, 'Could you tell me how—how it happened, please?'

Mrs Jackson refilled my glass.

'He used to sleep late, you know. He was a proper Bohemian, our Arnold. But I didn't like him laying in bed all morning. Well, it isn't nice, is it, with people coming in and out of the shop?'

I couldn't think why, but she seemed convinced about this point of social etiquette.

'So I always took him a cup of tea from our breakfast pot, to wake him up like. That very morning I went up at a half-past seven, and he said, "Don't let me sleep after nine, mother. I'm meeting somebody at ten." I should have known something was wrong. It wasn't like our Arnold to bother with appointments. That'd be last Tuesday. Eh, I can't believe it! Only last Tuesday.'

A ray of light shone momentarily at the edge of the nightmare. He had cared enough not to want to be late for our picnic.

'Poor Arnold,' said Mrs Jackson tearfully. 'In the midst of life he was in death.'

She began to sob and wipe her eyes with her apron, and Mr Jackson took up the tale.

'So mother went up just before nine, to wake him like he said. But the cup of tea was cold—and so was our Arnold.'

Then we all broke down. They were very kind to me. They said I would be welcome to call at any time, and they told me that when I felt better I could come and choose whatever I liked of his work.

'You can have anything of his,' said Mrs Jackson expansively, 'except Grandad's flower painting, of course. That's a Hairloom.'

I said, blowing my nose, 'Perhaps I'd better wait until term begins. He was quite a celebrity at the art school, you know. They'll probably put his work on exhibition. A few of the masters might want to choose a painting for their private collections. The Principal may have some pictures hung permanently in the school. . . .'

It is very difficult to change the views of a lifetime in a few moments, even under the duress of sudden death.

'You mean them . . . daubs?' Mr Jackson asked in a hushed voice, trying to be truthful and respectful at the same time.

Somewhat too late, I became Hannibal's publicity agent. They still did not understand, but they smiled and wiped their eyes and basked in his reflected glory. Mrs Jackson said that Arnold got it from his grandad but they had always encouraged him. She brought down grandad's flower painting as proof, and took credit for that as well.

'I wouldn't part with that picture for all the tea in China,' she said emphatically. 'It's a Hairloom.'

She had no such inhibitions about the disposal of her son's work, however, and was prepared to let the art school have the lot. To be fair to her, the whole matter was quite incomprehensible, and I think she had some vague idea that it was going to the nation. Then she put the kettle on and became practical with me.

'Now, love, you've had a bad shock. Let father strap your bicycle on top of the van and drive you home and explain to your mam and dad.'

I knew that I would be all right as long as I could churn those pedals round. If I had nothing to do but sit and think I should start crying again. And I could just picture my parents' reactions when I turned up in a grocer's van, and the grocer told them I had been in love with his son who was dead.

So I beat them off gently. And when I had washed my hands and face, and drunk strong tea, Mr Jackson wheeled out my bicycle for me in the same manner that a groom brings out a horse, and steadied the handlebars while I mounted. I felt better for tackling my problem by myself, and I cycled off in great style, but I don't remember much of the journey home.

How long had we known each other? Part of an autumn, a winter, a spring, most of a summer. Not quite a year. There would forever be weeks in my life which Hannibal Mundi had not blessed. There would be days which, for a long time, I could only remember as being anniversaries of his presence. I feared that my grief would be more cruel because less understood. My parents had never met him and would not have liked him. His parents were mourning for Arnold Jackson—a person who had, in a sense, never existed.

I possessed only one of his works, and that by accident, which I was housing for him during the vacation. It was a portrait of me, a painting in its first stages, recognisable but indistinct, light and insubstantial as a ghost. He had neither finished nor signed it, so it was of no value to anyone but me and I felt I could keep it. I had lugged it home lovingly on two buses at the end of the summer term, and now it was all I had left of him.

The unframed, unfinished canvas stood on a chest of drawers opposite the bed in my room. The light was gentler there, hiding its deficiencies, and I could see it when I woke up.

'What do you think of it?' I had asked my father hopefully.

Though no one could have thought of two more opposite families than mine and the Jacksons, the fact remains that they had a great deal in common. They were just as kind, just as narrow in a different way, and their children were enigmas to them. Still, they made the best of what must have been a bewildering situation.

'Is this something of yours?' my father asked tentatively.

I shook my head and said oh no, it was by someone far far better.

'Is it—finished?' he then asked, looking at it uncertainly.

He had been so often mistaken, and did not wish to offend.

I shook my head again. He was relieved. He blossomed. He became an art critic, glancing first at me and then back at it.

'Well, it bears a resemblance,' he said. 'At any rate I can see who it's meant to be. Yes, it captures the spirit of you,' he said.

I did not intend to confide in my parents, and I expected nothing from them in the way of deep sympathy. I decided I would say that a fellow student had died in case they wondered at my withdrawal, and look for comfort elsewhere.

I believed that no one had ever loved as well as we two, for all that our love affair was as unfinished as the portrait, but I needed reassurance. I wanted our friends to ring me up or write to me and say how sad they were, how lovely we had been together, what changes we had made to and for each other. No one did.

The autumn term had not yet begun. I stayed in my room and tried to screw up courage and contact those who had known us. In the end my nerve failed me. What had I to offer, after all, but my grief? And how much help would I need, for which I was too proud to ask? So my trouble detached me from the outside world, and the portrait was my only solace. In the absence of comfort, it comforted me.

Each morning I woke up and there it was, glimmering through the paint like a friend seen through fine veils. For when I put myself in Hannibal's position as painter, and looked through his eyes, I knew that he had seen and reached a truth of me known to no one else. For me he had laid aside his usual brilliant palette and chosen the most delicate colours; put away his palette knife and taken to fine brushwork; eschewed the *avant garde* in favour of the classical.

Each morning I found something new about it, something about myself which I had known but not understood before. Each morning it seemed clearer, and more defined. I began to realize that it was not simply an inner communion between myself and it. The portrait was still being painted. The paint gleamed fresh and bright. I touched the canvas. Nothing came away on my fingers.

Then I knew I was receiving a message from Hannibal Mundi.

I don't know why I hadn't thought of going back to the art school before, because he loved to stay behind and paint by himself, and the caretaker was used to keeping all hours. Even out of term they would allow students to work there by arrangement. And during term I sometimes stayed behind when Hannibal did, drawing still life in another room so as not to disturb his solitude. Then when Mr Mitchell began to cough and wander in and out and finger his keys, yearning to lock up, I found Hannibal and marched him off.

We used to buy fish and chips, and walk round the city eating them out of newspaper, and talking, and he always saw me safely onto the last bus home. So why hadn't I thought of it before?

It was that hour of a late September evening when the light is honeyed. The front door of the art school was standing slightly open, enough to welcome those who should be there and to deter those who should not. As I ran up the stairs and along the corridor towards the Life Room I nearly bumped into the caretaker, who was whistling softly and smiling to himself and jingling his keys.

'Sorry, Mr Mitchell!' I cried.

But he never minded any of us. He simply walked on, smiling, and whistling softly, and jingling his keys.

Then I stopped outside the open door because I felt in my bones that Hannibal was there. My hesitation rose from caution rather than fear because I didn't know anything about ghosts or how they behaved, except that they vanished at cock crow. So if I played my cards right we had the night to talk. I peeped round the nearest easel, hoping, and there he was: painting peacefully by himself in his corner, the honey-coloured light glinting on his broken glasses.

He must have sensed my presence too. He looked up, brush poised, and for a moment our awareness of each other hung in the quiet room.

Then he said, 'Don't be afraid, Miranda. Don't go away.'

I said, 'Oh, I'm not. Not in the least bit afraid, Hannibal. Just tremendously happy to find you. Can I come closer?'

He motioned to the model's dais, and I sat down at the edge, on the dusty velvet housecoat with which Doreen draped herself between sittings. Hannibal did not stop looking at me, and he swallowed as if something had happened which he wasn't too sure about, but wanted very much. He put down his brush and palette and sat on a chair opposite, and stuck his hands in the pockets of his jeans, looking and looking.

'So how's things?' we both said together, and laughed together, but the laugh wobbled and died.

'You look just as you used to look,' said Hannibal, 'but sadder.'

'So do you,' I said truthfully. 'I've never seen you look sad before. Actually, it quite suits you, Hannibal.'

Some spring in him had ceased to well. He was quieter, too.

'I expect it will take time to get over the first and worst of the separation,' he said. 'I know you're not to blame, but I didn't really expect you to up and leave me, Susie.'

I pointed to the breast of my T-shirt.

'*I* leave *you?*' I said indignantly. 'Damn me, Hannibal, you're the one who died!'

His scowl was so lifelike that I had to smile. Then the scowl straightened out and his expression became puzzled and kind.

'You've got two legs in one knicker, kiddo,' said Hannibal seriously. 'You're the one who died, not me.'

The room was silent with shock: a spectator, hands uplifted.

After a pause, I said, 'Hannibal, dearest of loves, you died in your sleep, on the morning we were supposed to meet for our picnic. I went over to your parents' shop and they told me. You were buried by the time I heard the news, Hannibal—not that I could have borne to go to your funeral anyway!'

He said, 'You actually spoke to my parents? And they told you I was dead?'

'Of a massive heart attack, your mother said. In your sleep. She said *massive* twice.'

He nodded. He recognized her style.

He said, 'I'll bet they gave me a terrific funeral.'

Then he sat for a while, looking at his hands and cracking his knuckles, thinking.

'What made you think *I* was dead?' I asked, when a decent interval had passed.

'On the morning we were supposed to go for our picnic,' he began, 'I overslept.' He corrected himself. 'I thought I had overslept. By the time I got to the bus stop you had gone. I thought you might have come here, but you hadn't. Then I heard somebody telling the caretaker that you'd been killed. You were riding on your bicycle with your head down and went slap into a lorry, near Belle Vue. Mustn't have known a thing about it. I was glad of that. Only I didn't quite know what to do next. That's why I didn't bother to go back to the shop. I've been here ever since. I thought that if I waited here you were bound to fetch up sooner or later.'

How many days had it been since I cycled over to Salford? And what had I been doing during those days? I couldn't remember talking to anyone, sleeping, eating. But I simply couldn't believe him.

'No, you're wrong. I'm still alive,' I said. 'I've been up in my room since I heard the news, sitting with your portrait of me. It's on the chest of drawers opposite my bed, and it's been such a comfort. But then it started to change. Each day it's becoming more substantial. I mean, this morning the hair was quite black. But it's there, and I've been with it, all the time, Hannibal. All the time.'

Hannibal got up and moved his easel round to face me. The portrait was there, glistening faintly with fresh paint. Finished.

I experienced again a fall into the void. The last time it had been for loss of Hannibal. Now it was for loss of myself.

'Did you cycle over to the shop?' he asked sympathetically.

I nodded.

'Then that's when it happened, my black-eyed

wench,' said Hannibal cheerfully. 'On the way home.'

He could see the funny side of death as well as life.

'Pedalling away. Heart-broken!' he said, grinning un-
ashamedly.

I glanced at him sideways. I saw it too.

'Blind with grief!' I added, straight faced.

We both started laughing.

'"And the sound of the waterfall, like *doom*!"' he
intoned. 'I say, Miranda, as you're a ghost too, and we
must be existing in some other dimension, do you suppose the dimension would mind if I gave you a kiss and a
hug?'

'Let's find out!' I said.

Perhaps it was because both of us were in the same
condition, because he felt as warm and bony and deli-
cious as ever.

'We're together, anyway,' Hannibal mumbled into my
long clean shining black hair. 'But, I say, Susie, what a
thing to happen to a lovely couple. Do you suppose we'll
be able to clank and groan and walk through walls?'

'I don't particularly want to. I wonder what happens
next?'

'Remember the Principal telling you not to tangle with
me, unless you had—what was it?'

'An insatiable desire for the unexpected and a life of
chaos!'

'He said it all. We've even had a death of chaos!'

'We might have another life. Or another sort of life.'

'Hey, we might meet up with Grandad and Grandma
Jackson!'

'I'd like that. What about the ones we don't want to
meet?'

'We'll float past and ignore them.'

'What shall we do now?'

'Walk round the city? Try to eat fish and chips? Haunt
mother? Who cares? It's time to go.' He struck an atti-

tude, crying, 'Where and how we know not, but we are met and something calls!' Then he sang in that swelling Italian tenor voice, 'Oh, come into the garden, Maud!'

I was glad that no one but myself could hear him.

I lingered by the painting, wondering what part it would play in the life we were leaving behind us.

'Hannibal, are there two of it? One at home, unfinished? One here, finished? Or is this a ghost, too?'

The girl on the canvas glowed with life. A quality I had seen in Grandad Jackson's flowers belonged to her. It showed great promise in some unspecified way. It would comfort anyone who had loved me.

Hannibal said seriously, 'I don't know, lass.'

Then he picked up his brush and signed the canvas anyway.

His Coy Mistress. Hannibal Mundi.